ONE KISS WILL DOOM HIM.
ONE BITE WILL CALM HER STORM.

SIREN'S KISS & FERAL BEASTS

ELENA M. REYES

SUMMARY

The Captain goes down with the ship…
Alpha Kai Daire is a pirate by necessity, and a predator by blood.
When the sacred heirloom his bloodline swore to protect vanishes
into the sea, he vows to return and reclaim his throne only when the
Cordis Lux is back in his grasp.
A year passes. Ports burn. And the blood on the Alpha's hands never
gets him closer—
Until he finds her again.
One Kiss dooms him.
One bite will calm her storm.
Nerissa Del Mare is the granddaughter of the mermaid king—
cunning, cloaked in magic, and hiding in plain sight. The tempting
little nymph is everything he's hunting, her song a call to his beast…
and the last thing he expected.
Their eyes meet, and the stone ignites—burns the brightest blue as
the universe orchestrates their inevitable collision. Because feral

need cannot be overridden by logic, and their bond will not be denied.

She's the key to his vengeance.

He's the ruin she was warned about.

And this time, the gods aren't just watching…

They demand a reckoning.

CONTENT WARNING

This book contains material that may be triggering for some readers.
It includes the following:

Violence & Death
Touch Her & Die
Sexism
FMC Is Hit By Family Member
FMC Treated Like Property (NOT MMC)
Explicit Sex
Blood Play
Werewolf (Monster)
Explicit Language
Biting/Mating Mark
Some Primal Play
Obsessive Anti-Hero
Knotting

GLOSSARY

WEREWOLVES:

- **Mind link** communications are in ***bold italic***.
- **Alpha King**: Ruler of all werewolf packs. Also referred to as alpha of alphas
- **Luna**: His Queen & Mate
- **Beta**: Second-in-command, but after the Luna
- **Gamma**: Third-in-command, also under the Luna
- **Pack**: Community of werewolves; family.
- **Moon Goddess:** The god who created the first shifter wolf and who they are devotees of.

HALF-SHIFT FORM:

- **Werewolf:** A rare form only the strongest alphas can control. They stand upright on two legs, with fur-covered bodies, sharp claws, and elongated fangs. Their face becomes a mix of human and wolf, showing the beast beneath the surface. This form allows both inhuman strength and strategy in battle.

- **Siren/Mermaid:** Small scales or translucent fins appearing on thighs, arms, or back when aroused, angry, or focused.

SIREN/MERMAID:

- **Siren's Song:** Primary weapon or a seduction tool. Can control, soothe, or manipulate emotions.
- **Tide-Hopper:** Anyone who doesn't live in the sea.
- **Clicking or Trilling:** Echo-like, underwater communication when in the presence of non-merpeople. Used for signaling or combat.
- **Mating Rite:** An ancient ritual that occurs once a mermaid comes of age and finds his or her mate. This goes beyond a bite. Jewelry is embedded into the flesh, symbolic of the bond and eternal claim.

Check out the Spotify Playlist for:
SIREN'S KISS & FERAL BEASTS.

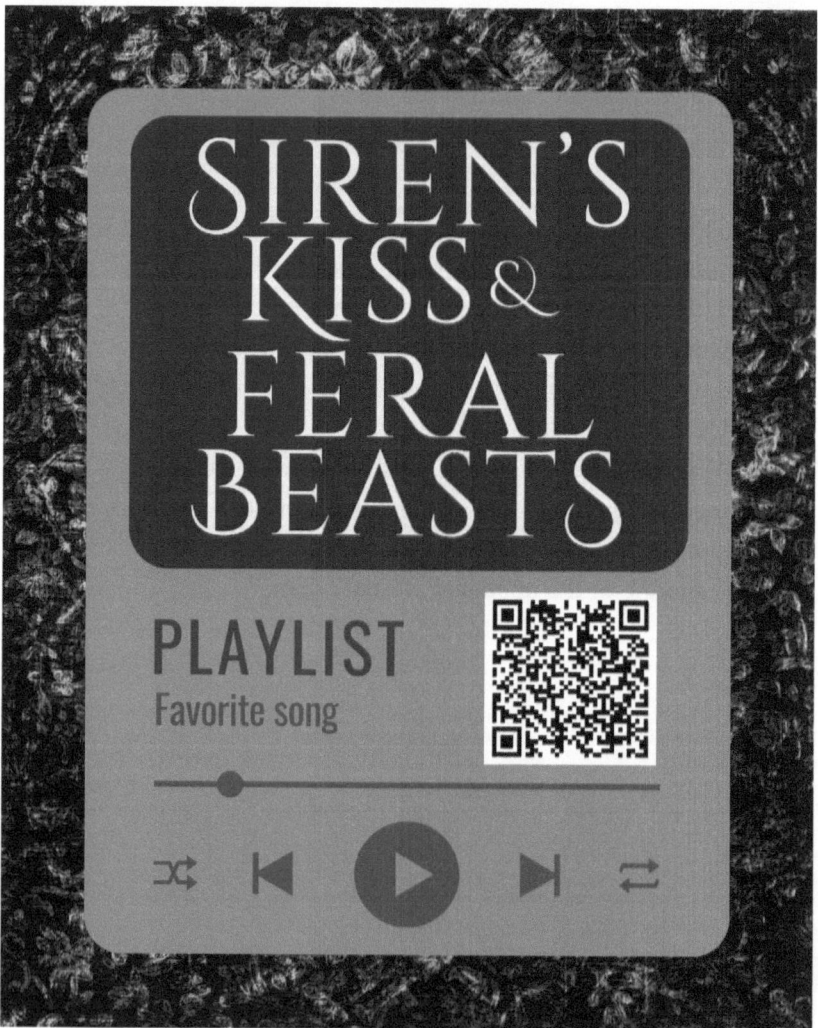

DEDICATION

*This ones for everyone obsessed with fated mates
who bite and lick and knot...*

We love a Feral King.

ONE **HUNDRED** YEARS AGO

GIFT & CURSE

ALPHA EPHRAIM DAIRE

"I'm sorry, my wolf."

Four words—simple and honest—and yet they rip my chest wide open and eviscerate the organ left exposed and at her mercy. Her denial doesn't just wound, it eviscerates, and my chest caves at her words. My ribs fracture beneath the weight of what she's done.

What she says she *must* do.

I'm still breathing. Still standing.

But I'm not alive.

I'm sorry, my wolf.

The lilt in her voice, so gentle—so full of sorrow—curls around my throat and strangles me.

I will never unhear those words. Not in this lifetime. Her pain is mine now, stitched into my marrow, and there's no undoing what's already begun.

I've lost my mate. The other half of my soul.

My wolf thrashes inside me as the truth sinks its poisonous claws in deep. He's calling for his female through the rough rumble building inside my chest, a pained purr for his mate to come back.

Accept our bite. Bear our pups. Grow old together while I live to worship her.

But now it will never be...

The divine bond between us cracks at the edges as the pull of her scent—once heady and lush with sea-kissed fruit—begins to fade. Each second, it grows fainter. Each second, my desperation grows feral.

Everything in me, in my soul, demands that I pick her up and run away.

I'd followed her siren's call across the beach tonight.

She'd risen from the depths, a silver mist curling around her luminous form like a second skin. I watched reverently as pearly pink scales recede from her thighs, revealing skin kissed by the moonlight. Her gown is almost translucent, revealing every inch of skin I ache to kiss and nip and memorize.

She came with no pretense.

"I do not accept your rejection, Princess," I manage through clenched teeth, my tone rough. Final. Desperate. "You are my gift from the goddess, and I will not forsake you."

Tears track down her cheeks, her bottom lip trembling, and yet, her spine is made of steel. Straight and unyielding. *She would've been the perfect luna. We could've united the kingdoms and ruled together.* "And yet...we can never be, Alpha Ephraim."

My name on her plump lips is both heaven and hell. A gift and a curse.

How am I supposed to live a lifetime without hearing this again?

"Why, Lucienne? Why are you breaking our hearts?" The question rips itself from my chest, a growl heavy with agony. Man and wolf, we bleed into one—my canines drop and I throw my head back, howling the injustice at the moon. My insides are shredded and bleeding, starving for the one thing the gods promised and fate cruelly stole. "Answer me."

Claws tear through my palms, my talons dripping blood onto the white sandy beach. I want the pain, welcome it, while behind us, the waves crash. The warm blue waters, where I feel most at home, don't bring me comfort tonight. Instead, I stare out at the parted stretch, exposing the floor below.

It feels desolate. As empty as I feel.

Not a single fish or creature can be seen, and I know this is her doing.

Her family rules the ocean, while mine rules the land above.

A wolf and a siren. *She's my perfect match.*

"Please forgive me, my alpha," Lucienne says, her voice hoarse and heavy with pain. The heir to the merpeople's crown stands regal, the bottom hem of her long and flowy white dress soaked while light pink scales appear at her temples and collarbones, the moon's light reflecting like opals. *So fucking beautiful.* "This arrangement was made before my birth. To protect—"

"Who are you protecting? From what?" Garbled, the words slip past the knot in my throat. Past the devastation of knowing I could have kept her safe if we had met earlier.

"You." At her response, my mind reels and my body goes cold. I'm struggling to piece together the fragments of truth she's given me. Her eyes flicker with guilt and sorrow. Then there's also a sliver of something darker—as if she's trying to rein in her ire...

For my sake. For hers.

Yet before I can ask *why,* she takes in a deep breath and lets it out slowly. "They wanted a merman to rule, Ephraim, not a queen. They feared what I'd become; my power, your bloodline—we would tear down kingdoms and rule as equals. My father didn't want that." Her voice cracks, the last word catching in her throat. "He wanted the patriarchy to thrive, and so did the general. They threatened to kill you and your family—"

"How long?" I ask, stepping toward her with clenched fists.

I'm fighting the urge to pull her into me, *hold her tight,* and tell her everything will be okay. But I can't. She took that from me. "How long have you known I'm your fate? That you were my gift?"

I want to kill whoever touched what's rightfully mine. Tear out the bite marks my mate gave him.

"Ten years."

"Ten years," I repeat, closing my eyes as the wolf inside me howls in sorrow. The anger, the betrayal—it's almost too much to contain. *She chose my life over our love.* "We can fix this."

My canines thrum with the need to mark her elegant neck, to bind her to me in every way a wolf welcomes and accepts his fated mate, but Lucienne shakes her head. As if she knows what I'm thinking—what I want—my beautiful siren takes a few steps closer to the shoreline.

Lucienne Del Mare, heir to the sea, stands regal in her sorrow as the distance between us grows. A queen among mortals; I'd give my life to worship and build kingdoms of salt and stone in her honor. She would've been my home. My solace, after a lengthy voyage across wolfen lands.

The other half of my soul.

"What's done cannot be undone, Ephraim Daire. My daughter loves her father, and I will not break her heart."

"Instead, you tore mine."

"I'm sorry, but I choose them."

She was meant to be mine, and I was ready to give her everything.

A luna to rule by my side.

A goddess to match my alpha's soul.

Our bond should've been unbreakable and undeniable.

And yet, this is what I get in return...

Silence. Grief. A stolen choice.

A muscle ticks in my jaw, and I'm fighting back my instincts that demand I take her. That we end this betrayal the only way we know how, through claiming what's ours, but then she lifts a delicate hand... I freeze. "Don't, my siren."

"You were the only thing I ever wanted for myself, my wolf. Selfishly and unapologetically..." Lucienne whispers, eyes closing for a second before meeting mine, full of regret and sorrow, "...but I was not born to want. I was born to give."

"You were mine before you were ever his."

"And that will never change." The air between us grows heavy as the final threads of our frayed bond unravel one by one, until all that's left is the echo of what could've been. With shaky fingers, she removes a gold chain from around her delicate neck and pries my clawed fist open before placing the onyx stone at the center. Then her palm covers mine, and the heat from the gem burns an imprint onto my flesh.

It hurts, but the pain is dull compared to what I've lost.

From the darkest black to a fiery blue shines between our joined hands as her dress rips and her scales rise. Every inch of her curvaceous body is laid bare for me, and an intricate pattern of iridescent pink shimmers under the moon's light, a haze that swirls around us now before she pulls her touch from mine. The mist disappears over the jewel.

It's back to black. No more blue.

The feel of her magic is a wondrous thing. Her tethers felt like an old friend, someone I used to know but lost contact with over the years.

She's beautiful, but not mine. Not anymore.

"The Cordis Lux stone is my gift to you, Ephraim." A cooling jolt settles over my palm, and a flicker of azure appears. Then, it dies. "A part of my magic will always belong to you, as it should, and this will protect you."

"It's not what I want."

"I know." She nods solemnly. Her violet eyes flash with hurt, but that too disappears quickly. "But I needed you to have this. Know that you'll always be safe."

Slowly, I close my fist around the stone before slipping it into my trouser pocket. The act is deliberate, like I'm sealing a door that should never have been open, before I take a step back.

My chest aches, my body trembling with the force of everything I'm forced to accept. "You will never see me again, Lucienne," I grind out, and the words taste like ash in my throat. "There's no going back from this."

A tear spills from her violet eyes. Her lips tremble, and yet...she smiles. Not cruelly. Not kindly. Just *acceptance*. "So be it, my wolf. I deserve no less."

"I will never look for you in the waters I travel through."

"Just as mermaids will never sing for wolves." Lucienne turns away then. She walks into the sea, and the water welcomes her like a lover. Protective. Reverently. Her ethereal eyes never meet mine again, and before I can say her name one last time, she disappears beneath the waves.

Our vows are all we have left of our bond.

May the gods one day forgive us and our bloodlines never pay the price...

Alpha
Kai

PROLOGUE

*"*T*he captain always goes down with the ship."*

She drags her sharp, luminescent nails down the front of my trousers, shredding the fabric and zipper just enough to free my cock. It springs free, and I'm throbbing; the engorged head's dripping pre-come while her nose skims me from the slit down to my heavy knot.

There, she pauses and breathes me in.

Her soft lips are a gift, while the bite of her nails on my skin—her full-body shivers—causes my wolf to growl in approval. Nerissa's scent deepens at that, at how close my beast is to the surface, and the natural sweetness of her slick takes on a sharper note as it surrounds us.

A little earthier. More decadent.

My body throbs with need, yet I remain still as both sides of me take in her every movement. My wolf is proud of his treacherous mate, and I find her actions amusing. Adorable.

How she stole from me and then ran is our primal dance.

How she tied me to the ship's mast is foreplay.

"I'm famished, my wolf," my mate croons, looking up at me from beneath her long, dark lashes. Her violet eyes are hooded while her small, yet sharp fangs bite into her bottom lip. "Will you feed me?"

"You're playing a dangerous game, little treasure."

"You don't scare me, Alpha."

"I live to protect you, Nerissa Del Mare. I'd never harm you."

"Then give me what I need, Alpha Daire." Her lips brush across the tip of my cock. The act is reverent and sweet, while the heat in her violet eyes promises a painful reckoning. One soft kiss. One whispered vow. "Feed my selfish desire and need, Wolf. What I'm begging for."

The last word hasn't fully left her sinful mouth before Nerissa flicks her tongue across the engorged head, paying extra attention to the slit where drops of pre-come bead for her. Her hum at my taste is like an electrical shock to my knot—I throb and swell in her tiny hand while she tightens her grip. Those delicate fingers don't meet around my girth. Her mouth stretching over the head looks obscene, but then nothing else registers.

Slow. Wet. Merciless.

Velvet-soft lips wrap around me, working me deeper in small, yet quick bobs of her head until I kiss the back of her throat. Then, there's the scrape of her sharp nails digging into my thighs—the bite of pain is driving my wolf mad, and it's taking every ounce of self-control I possess not to fuck her throat.

To not tear off these pathetic shackles and take control.

I'm allowing my mate this one moment of victory before hunting and mounting my prey. It's in a wolf's biology to toy with its food before tearing into its flesh, and I plan to indulge this beautiful siren until it's my turn to *bite*.

Chains rattle above me, my muscles trembling from the absolute savagery building inside as Nerissa's perfect mouth sucks me. She can't take the full length, but we have the rest of our lives to fix that. To train her to take my knot there, too.

"More," she moans around my girth, her eyes fluttering closed as she savors my taste. The vibrations feel so fucking good, and my chest rumbles with approval while she hollows her cheeks. The look on her face is pure bliss, as if she were praying for mercy and repentance simultaneously—I smile.

There is no escaping my wrath when this is all said and done. *She'll pay for this with her cunt, right before I take her ass. Fair trade after stealing from me.* Because we both know how easily I could snap both these chains and her neck, although I'd never hurt her.

Never her. Anyone but her.

A small string of drool runs down the corner of her mouth and chin, marking the scales still exposed across her collarbone. I grunt at the sight. At the blood there, too. My blood. The deep gouges her nails made on my flesh have dirtied her, and it only serves to heighten her beauty.

Filthy. Sinful. Perfection.

"When this is over, I'm going to give you the world, my female." A promise. My vow. But then the ship groans beneath us; a deafening crack forms a few feet from where she's sucking my cock. We're sinking, and fast—the shouts from my crew break through the raging storm. They call my name, beg me to get off the ship and get to safety, but I don't move.

I'd never ruin her fun. And my female is enjoying herself while ignoring the damage she's created.

The obscene sound of her gagging on my length is worth my ruined ship ten times over.

"Motherfuck," I hiss out from between clenched teeth as her throat spasms, tightly stroking my cock with each swallow. One of my clawed hands embeds itself into what's left of the mast while the other uses the limited mobility the shackle gives me to wrap her hair around my fist.

Grip tight, I keep her in place but don't thrust my hips. Instead, I enjoy the quick bob of her throat on each swallow and the bite of her *nails* as they once again pierce my flesh. The more the vessel tips, flooding each floor, the more aggressive—desperate—my little storm becomes.

The ship tilts further, and a few crates smash against each other. They shatter upon impact, fragments scattering—banging on everything in their path—and yet my mate never stops taking me in deep.

When a small piece of glass from a now broken window slices across my abdomen, I feel her shiver as the air becomes tinged with my blood and need. Her mouth works me harder, deep strokes, before pulling back and licking a path from tip to knot and then to the cut on my stomach.

Both man and beast snarl at her.

Chest heaving. Canines flashing. Drops of pre-come falling to the floor...

The little nymph only smirks at me. "Behave, Wolf."

That's it. Just the directive to stay compliant while Nerissa gazes at the already healing small wound. She follows the movement of each drop and then completely shatters me by licking each one clean. Her tongue is so fucking soft as it slides across the cut, but it's the tingling sensation left behind that causes a hard shiver to rush through me. It's almost volatile; my muscles clench and unclench while my knot swells to near painful.

Her scales, beautiful in their varying shades, also begin to vibrate. The movement is subtle, and the pulse is rhythmic in a pattern of three and four counts between short pauses—I'm entranced. It's a language I don't understand yet, but that I plan to become a scholar of.

"That's my beautiful treasure. Such a good little female worshipping her mate."

At my praise, Nerissa flashes me a sweet look before taking me back into her hot little mouth. Each bob of her head is fast while one hand skims fingers across my knot and lower, squeezing my heavy balls hard enough to sting, but the bite of pain and pleasure only makes me harder.

My release is so close. She can tell, too, and gives the heavy sack a sharp tug.

I release my grip on her hair as water laps at our feet and then our shins. Everything feels in slow motion; the wet heat of her mouth distracts me from the ship's destruction and the worry of my pack members on longboats somewhere nearby. There's not a single fuck in me about the waves crashing and forcing us into what feels like a whirlpool, or the way lightning strikes the wreckage as it drifts out.

All I see and acknowledge is her.

My female. My mate.

Nerissa transforms slowly, her tail shimmering beneath the water, now reaching my knees. What's left of the mast groans, and I do too as she flicks the end back and forth, staying right where I need her.

"Mine."

"I'm yours, Nerissa. Take what you need."

"Never forget that, Alpha," she says, and this time, when she sucks me in, Nerissa doesn't stop until reaching my knot. There, she tightens her lips and teases the underside with the tip of her tongue...

"Fuck," I hiss out from between clenched teeth as the first rope of my spend lands on her tongue. She hums in appreciation at that, hollowing her cheeks and bobbing—milking every last drop. And sexier than anything this gorgeous siren has done...?

The blush on her face as she looks up at me with those violet eyes and swallows.

Perfection. Home. Mine.

Pulling back, she kisses the tip a final time and rises to lay a tiny nip to my bottom lip. Her small fangs cut the skin, her cherry lips now stained with my blood and come as a sharp snap rends the air.

That sound is—

Goddess, everything comes back into focus as I take in a full breath. The late-night sky is lit up with the storm, and rain begins to pelt hard just as the water reaches my chest. The weight of the broken mast is dragging me down, dark water surrounding me, and yet I see it all.

The flash of pain on her face as she slips beneath the water.

The gleam of metal around my wrist.

The light coming from something just past the isolated storm…

And then it's all black. Endless black, until a lithe form swims past me and small fingers skim across my skin. It's a shock to my senses and my beast—the electrical tethers of our bond and the bite of pain as she rips the Cordis Lux from around my neck. My wolf is present in my glowing eyes, taking in the way her clan swims away —they surround their princess—but her movements aren't as fluid.

She's fighting every inch of space between us.

It's there in the lackluster sway of her beautiful tail and rigid shoulders. Slow, as if it physically pains her to swim away from me, but just as they move past the wreckage, she turns a final time, and our eyes meet. I'm growling deep, and the vibrations carry through the water to her.

My mate shivers and extends her right hand out toward me, then pulls it back as I snap each shackle off. Now, there's a hint of nervousness in her expression, and in the semi-formed bond, there's a tug of trepidation for my next move.

And to her surprise, there isn't one. Not yet.

For now, I want her to swim away and hide. I want to earn the right to mount my female.

I'm going to disprove every lie they've fed her.

I will conquer the sea—destroy those separating us—leaving no shelter except me.

I am her home. All she'll ever need.

I'm coming for you, my sinful treasure. There's no escaping me.

Alpha
Kai

ONE

ONE YEAR AGO...

"*Shadow born. Blood forged. Shadow born. Blood forged.*"

Wolves chant as I move through the crowd, making my way toward the center of the fighter's circle. Some pound their chests in unison, gazing straight ahead, while others drop to one knee with their heads bowed. Both are a show of respect as their howls pierce the night, echoing through the open field not far from the island's shore—an ancient call that seals their loyalty to me.

Their king. Their Alpha.

"*Shadow born. Blood forged. Shadow born. Blood forged.*"

The ground beneath my bare feet is wet and warm. The trail of blood and sand—the unconscious bodies of territory leaders being dragged through on their way to the healer's tent—is a testament to our ancient ways. It's tradition. A sacred ritual.

I've held it for the last four years, since taking over as alpha. Just as my father did before me.

The victor of the previous fight retakes his place in the audience, limping and bruised, his head bowed in my direction while I take in the damage inflicted.

Two broken palm trees, snapped in half.

Ripped fur and fragments of skin on the eroded ground.

Sanguine stains feed the earth beneath our feet as the goddess is paid her dues.

Every wolf here has earned his place through dominance, blood, and fire. Many have challenged me and lost over the last few years— leaders in their own right with packs they're responsible for—but here, they kneel.

My word is law. Their loyalty is to me. To our brotherhood.

Pirates. Wolves. Bloodthirsty.

Tonight, though, a few seek to settle old grudges. Others want favor from the royal house.

No matter the reason, they've come because I commanded it.

The summit is mandatory.

No excuse. No mercy.

Once a year, male and female commanders from different corners of the five seas converge on this consecrated isle. It started when my grandfather fought his king in a challenge, then was carried on by my father, and it will not die under my rule.

Our wolves, the other half of us, demand a reckoning.

Not politics. Not alliances.

We are beasts wrapped in skin, ruled by dominance and truth. Two souls in one body. And while we may walk on two legs, speak in tongues, and rule like men...

The wolf always lingers beneath the surface.

"Shadow born. Blood forged. Shadow born. Blood forged."

They're louder now. Thirstier. Their chants and howls intertwine with the lightning strike not far from where I stand. It lands in the dark water, maybe thirty feet from the shoreline, but the effect ripples throughout. The ground trembles and electricity pulses in my veins, and the latter has nothing to do with the storm.

My wolf is restless. On alert.

Something feels off...

Pack leaders close the circle once I step through, leaving an open ring of sand for the next battle to begin. The air is heavy with the scent of rain as two worlds collide, and I'm addicted to the mix.

Wet earth and salty sea.

One is my home, while the other beckons me closer. The pull is getting stronger every day.

"Final challenge," I say, my voice carrying through the crowd, and every leader steps back, except one man. He's not a commander, much less a member of my kingdom, and I tilt my head to the side, studying him as he steps inside the ring with me.

He's thin, dirty, and missing a front tooth. His hair is matted, the color of rust.

But more than that is his scent.

Putrid. Dishonest. *Criminal.*

The difference between him and a pirate like me? I have a moral code, even if it is small.

We don't hurt women. We don't steal from the defenseless.

Something rogue wolves don't abide by. He's also not the kind who voluntarily leaves his or her pack for a solitary life among humans. There's no thread or bond to his previous home. No mating mark that explains his decision to live away from the sanctity of a pack.

Not that it couldn't happen. Choosing to leave is uncommon, but it has happened because of love or the simple need for change—yet a tether always remains. Those wolves maintain a connection to their birth family and each pack member. They're also welcomed back anytime with open arms, but this man...

There's nothing honest in his cold, lifeless eyes. In the small tremble of his hand, one that conceals a sharp blade under his lightly tattered sleeve. *Strike one.*

"What territory do you represent, Wolf?" I ask as my beast stretches within me, pushing against my skin to be let out while my fangs descend. They tear through the gums and cut my bottom lip; I taste the metallic and smile. "Answer me."

He swallows hard at the sight, but doesn't retreat. "I'm a southerner—"

"Lies!" three men shout in unison. It's a father and his sons, their faces contorted in outrage, yet their necks bend low in apology for the disruption. The older male takes one step forward, though, keeping his body a few inches outside of the ring while holding up a hand. "Please forgive us, my alpha. May I speak freely?"

I nod once. "Go on."

"Thank you." Turning his head, his eyes zero in on the rogue, and whatever show of respect had been given to me is gone. This pack leader is repulsed—anger flows out from him, and it's directed at the man standing across from me. The latter staggers a bit but manages to remain upright. "He is *not* one of my pack members. My wolf doesn't recognize him, and his scent is that of—"

"I am from the south," the rogue interjects, his voice trembling with rage. "Do not speak for me. Do not lie."

"You insolent, filthy—" I shake my head at the furious old wolf, and he cuts himself off. Even his sons, who'd been snarling low, stop.

"Rogues have no place here. Especially ones who lie."

"Where I go is my decision, *Your Majesty.* Not yours." *Disrespect number two.*

"Watch yourself, or I might take your idiocy as a challenge."

He takes a single step forward, chest puffing out a bit. "And if it is?"

I smile. "Then so be it."

Lightning crashes just off the coast, lighting up the black sky a second before the first drop of rain falls on my forehead. This storm's been brewing all evening off the horizon with its dark clouds and flashes of light—the loud clap of thunder intertwining with the chants of my wolves.

Because they don't like intruders, and that's what this lone shifter is.

A grifter with no loyalty or bonds, two things wolves need.

Pack is family. Pack is sacred.

"Name your terms, rogue," I growl, baring my teeth at the smaller man who dared to step into the circle with me. Although, I'll give him credit for not tucking his tail. Most do when in my presence. "What do you want?"

"You, my king." His voice isn't loud, but it carries, and I tilt my head to the side. Take note of his subtle, yet defiant sneer. "I'm here to challenge you for the title of alpha of all alphas."

His declaration is met with anger. Exiled wolves are not to be trusted, and with good reason; this one carries the stench of betrayal. Hunger for power.

But more than that, he's brought with him three other wolves...

The rogue's eyes shift from side to side, looking for something, and he exhales roughly when two males and a small female come into view. They're scared as they walk closer to the circle; I can smell the fear coming from all three, but they don't run away. Instead, they quietly huddle closer and pull a small spray bottle from the woman's bag.

I'm not the only one who notices, as my beta and gamma scent the air. Not that they find anything, and there's only one way for a shifter—rogue or pack—to hide their presence:

Scent blockers.

Not a new concept. It's a tactic used in battle when trying to surprise an opponent, but to use it here is the definition of stupid. Or maybe cocky. However, the better question is...

How the fuck did they get past the guards on patrol?

My beta, Veris, moves closer while my gamma, Torren, takes his position directly to the left of me. Both are in my line of sight. Both are poised to attack, but I give a minute shake of my head.

The male intruders don't catch the directive, but the woman does, and her mouth opens. No words come out. She's frozen, drops the bottle, but the man to her right catches it, muttering under his breath about her *fucking shit up.*

He's wrong. That would be them.

Keep an eye on them. No harm to the woman.

The mindlink message is sent to both Veris and Torren. In return, I get a quick: **Yes, Alpha.**

Don't trust them. Scared wolves don't challenge alphas, Torren adds a moment later, while Veris flashes his canines at the trio. They whimper, the noise setting off multiple snarls across the beach.

Looking back at the challenger, I raise a brow. "Name."

He swallows hard, hand clenching around the blade he's trying to conceal. "Spiro."

"Spiro, what?"

"No last name. I've renounced it."

"Last. Name," I ask from behind clenching teeth. "I won't ask again."

"Marros. Spiro Marros."

He wasn't lying. The name Marros originated in the south, in Mar De Juramentos Rotos or *Sea of Broken Oaths*, and they're all watchers. Long line of them; they live and maintain lighthouses or towers on high elevations near the shore to help guide fleets home or warn of incoming storms. Respectable, the job comes with good pay and trust from the pack, but from the disdain on his face, it's not enough for him.

My eyes shift toward the elder leader, and his brows are furrowed. "Is he lying?"

Confusion is clear on his face, but the elder commander nods. "It's true, Alpha. Marros's son was exiled..." he pauses, and I wave a hand for him to carry on "...but this man looks nothing like his father or his offspring."

"I am him, not that it matters—"

"It doesn't." Both look at me, but my focus is on Spiro. "The challenge stands."

"I'm ready."

"Beta, start the countdown." Immediately, the ground vibrates—the stomping of angry beasts travels through me, and I respond with a growl that further ignites their thirst for blood. Those who watched the earlier fights through their wolf's eyes shift, their hands now pounding their chests.

Solidarity. Family. Pack. Everything Spiro Marros doesn't understand or value.

It's our way of life, and hierarchy isn't guaranteed by birth. It's earned. It's valued.

And while my family has ruled for three generations, we have fought and killed to keep our crown. Alphas are challenged—threatened—and losing a battle comes with consequences bigger than the control of territory.

Every fight comes with a sacrifice. No exceptions.

Money. Land. Mates, in some rare instances, when the fight is over a woman or a man.

However, this time I'll collect more than whatever meager possessions Spiro owns.

Only one of us will walk out of this ring alive.

ALPHA
KAI

TWO

"Go easy on him, Alpha," Veris calls out, and others around him snort. The sound is a mix of annoyance meets amusement, and I throw a smirk at my friend.

"Not in my nature, Beta, but…" I trail off, my ear picking up the scrape of sand as Spiro shifts into a fighting position. *Why is he doing this?* Because it's not for honor, much less misplaced worry over his wolfen brethren. Not even his greed can cover the stench of fear that's too thick to ignore.

"Fight me!" Spiro yells out what he considers a warning, growl slipping through. To me, though, it's more like the yip of a pup. Not menacing in the least. Almost laughable.

"Attack at the sound of the horn." Giving him my back, I slip my shirt over my head. It's tossed somewhere to my right, just grazing the floor, when a smaller body slams into my back.

Then *he* falls back onto his ass.

Me? I don't move.

No budge or shift, Spiro's force is that of a gnat, and for a minuscule moment, I pity the idiot. He's no match for me, and we both know it.

Taking in a deep breath, I stretch my neck from side to side. Let him regroup for a minute or two while reigning in my wolf.

For his benefit, not mine.

"Face me," he snaps, the attempt at a command quite comical if nothing else. "Man to man."

I ignore him. My attention is elsewhere...

My nostrils flare as the scent of orange blossoms and coconut, with the light undertone of vanilla, sweeps over me on a gentle breeze. My reaction is automatic; every muscle in my body expands before clenching tight, a heaviness in my knot that I can't ignore. Hunger unlike anything I've experienced lashes across my senses, and I shake my head to try and clear the haze.

Sweet and floral; I want more. Wolf and man, we feel a tug—a call that's impossible to ignore.

Who the fuck owns that mouthwatering scent?

Another deep inhale, and I close my eyes. Savor the moment as the world stops and the stone pendant on my chain warms for a second before growing ice cold. Here and then gone, and I turn my head toward the water when the scent vanishes.

It's in that momentary distraction that I seem to deeply offend the rogue.

He shouts something I don't pay a lick of attention to. Comes closer, but it's when his hand grips my arm that I whirl on him, lips peeled back over my teeth. "Remove your filthy hand." I'm angry at his audacity, but more so at the loss of that glorious perfume.

"Then fight me." Spiro's body is tense as he takes a few steps back, the glint of metal more pronounced now as he flicks the butterfly knife fully open. He tightens his grip. His eyes nervously shift away from me for a second, his attention toward the rogues with him before making his final mistake.

The last one he'll ever make.

Spiro lunges, blade high, and my beast surges forward with an instant half shift. My clawed feet drag across the sand as I sidestep his sloppy charge, grabbing him by the throat and slamming him spine-first into the ground. The knife slips from his hand and lands with a muted thud partially buried beneath sand, while the air cracks from the impact.

An audible gasp leaves the female rogue seconds after; I understand why.

A small mist of blood spreads in the wind as he chokes, his smaller hands trying to pry my claws from his skin—he fails. Instead, I dig them in a little deeper. The beast and I revel in the way his muscles tear as if my claws were a knife slicing through butter. Almost no force needed, and the sight of him squirming like a worm is amusing.

Tilting my head to the side, I grin. "You have a choice, Spiro. One I don't give most people..."

"Get the fuck off!" he cries out, trying to use his feet to kick me away, and once again fails miserably. *Pathetic.*

"I'm truly disappointed, mutt." Lowering my face to his, I unleash the tight grip on my alpha's aura, and Spiro cries out. Dominance radiates from me, a presence every shifter—member of my pack or rogue—acknowledges. It slithers around them, demands they yield to my command, and the physical manifestation of my bark is in the bending of spines and neck—it digs its claws into their instincts and tells them who I am.

What will happen if I'm defied...

This is the perfect example of such an act.

His challenge is met by force, and Spiro Marros finds himself pinned with my claws seconds from ripping his throat out.

"Who sent you, rogue? How did you get here?"

"I don't—"

"Liars never make it into the goddess' presence, Spiro. Tell me,"

I growl out, voice deep, and the finality of the command is unyielding. Defying me will hurt him and his wolf, the latter of which is trying hard to break free but can't. Spiro tries to half-shift, but the glitch between animal skin and human skin distorts before leaving a panting mess beneath my grip.

Instead of defeat, he tries one last attempt to switch to fur.

His claws slip in and out, his wolf's coat emerging then fading across trembling limbs. It's a draining process to find the right balance between the two forms, and only those with the alpha's power have been able to control it for the past century.

We have movement from the two male rogues, Kai. To your left, but outside the ring. Torren's message comes in as I bare my elongated fangs, mouth open to tear off flesh.

All three on their knees. No one moves. No one leaves.

Yes, Alpha.

"Tell me who you're working for, and I'll make sure your next miserable attempt at a shift is your last." At my command, his wolf cowers while the human clenches his jaw, fighting the need to bow his spine.

"You're no real king, Kai Daire."

Silence. His statement is met with complete and utter silence.

My answer to that? I let him go. My claws retract slowly, fingers flexing so the wounds widen and blood bubbles at the surface of each gouge before slipping down the side of his neck and onto the sand. The stains are vivid under the moon, the gentle rain only spreading the color until an imprint of his neck is left behind.

One that becomes visible to everyone once he stands after *I* step back a few feet.

Spiro's hand cups his neck, checking the injuries while a smirk spreads across his face. "Did that sting, Your Majesty? The truth usually does."

Gasps ripple at this man's blind ignorance.

Because I'm not known for my patience or for showing leniency, and this mutt has tugged the wrong beast's tail. Wolves around the world heed my warning—know that both animal and man thirst for blood, and to some degree, so do these wolves here in attendance. Violence is in our blood, the same way a siren's song will lead mortals to their death.

"You talk too fucking much for a dead wolf, Marros."

"Fuck you!" Spiro stumbles forward, his arm cocked back, and throws a messy punch. It's desperate and wild, and I catch his closed fist mid-air, twisting it hard enough that a pop rends the air. The dislocation of bone echoes, but not louder than the scream it rips from his throat.

Then I return the favor; the difference is that my attacks land in precise succession.

A knee to the ribs, chest, and then face. Blood flies like a fine mist, the drops sliding down my tattooed chest, while my claws rip into him without pause, and a chunk of his shoulder lands near his now kneeling companions. Someone gags, while a sorrowful cry rends the air.

Deafening, and yet, I can make out each pained noise leaving the rogue.

"Did that hurt?"

"No." Not as cocky.

Laughter bubbles out of me, loud and boisterous, but it dies as fast as it arrives. "You think you're owed something?"

"Fuck—" he pauses to spit out a fragment of tooth, stumbling; I drag him up by the collar before slamming him into the trunk of a thick palm ten feet away. Bark splinters. Prongs fall along with a few coconuts, adding insult to injury. The last one splits his forehead open.

"Watch your words."

"When I'm king, I'll make every last wolf here bow and kiss my feet."

"What makes you think you're better than every pack leader here who's challenged me and lost?"

"Because you'll answer the call and lose. No one's infallible."

"What call? Who the hell sent you?" Yet, as the last question slips through my gritted teeth, that scent floods my senses again. This time, it's stronger. Fragile, yet the layered dominance of a sweet floral aroma makes my cock harden. My balls grow swollen and heavy.

A howl rips from my chest, full of something I've never felt before...

Longing.

Savage hunger.

I drop Spiro like garbage before landing another blow, this time a closed fist to his gut, and the asshole folds in half. The sound of angry waves crashing onto the shore catches my attention, and I once again give him my back. He's no threat to me, but my wolf's senses are drawn to the sea, and the pull is getting stronger by the second.

The animal rises to the surface, and through his eyes we watch the light storm intensify, and what minutes ago was a misting rain turns into thunder. Heavy drops begin to fall, too. Violent and fast; a demand we heed its warning.

Keep an eye on the shoreline.

Both my beta and gamma confirm they heard, and I sense their movements, the buzz of conversation with my guards to prepare. For what? I have no clue, but we're not alone tonight.

"Make your move, or I'll end this quickly." The lax way I render the threat angers him, and Spiro tries to shift but fails. His wolf is cowering; the mangy thing recognizes the bigger predator, even if I haven't fully unleashed my beast yet. I don't have time for his nonsense, and those around us sense the change in me.

Power is dangerous when wielded by those who crave it. Because there's a difference between earning it—studying those who came before you—and demanding it. I rule for my people, not for my pocket or the accolades. I kill for the same reasons.

To protect. To serve.

Spiro's mind is clouded by a false sense of entitlement, and tonight it's his downfall.

"Shadow born. Blood forged. Shadow born. Blood forged."

The chants start again, and this time, they're louder. Demand retribution.

This fuels him. His anger and hatred morph—control his reactions—and the idiot lunges for my throat, the knife in his hand again. "I'll show you all!"

When he picked it up, I don't know or care. The second he's close, I shift. The blade grazes my shoulder mid-turn, but it's too late for him. My jaw clamps down and shakes, teeth embedded deep in his ribs. Bones crack. A few pierce through the skin, flooding my mouth with blood. Each sanguine drop tastes as rancid as his soul, and I release him for a minute and just watch.

My ears pick up his wheeze.

His movements slow.

I give him the choice to bleed out silently and with some dignity, but he chooses to attack. Before he can grip the handle of his weapon, I jump on him. His back hits the wet sand, a pain-filled yowl filling the night as his wounds rip open further.

My wolf towers over the dying rogue.

It's inevitable. His penance.

My claws dig into Spiro's torso, the cut sharp and unforgiving—my weight crushing his chest, slowly adding pressure until my paws become wet and tinged with red. A low whine escapes his throat the deeper I dig. It's a sign of submission, but the feral anger in his eyes turns to hope as he focuses on something—someone toward the shore.

Not that it matters. No one can save him.

With a vicious growl, I raise my blood-soaked paw and bring it down hard. There's a crack, and his eyes widen; his lips part in a scream that never escapes as his heart gives way beneath the force.

He's dead, vacant eyes on the shore, and I follow their line of sight.

Feminine silhouette. Flowing dark hair. *That same mouthwatering scent.*

It hits me with the weight of a thousand-pound boulder…

"Son of a bitch."

Every cell in my body contracts. It's a painful blow to my wolf as he goes from feral to almost docile as he recognizes what this means.

What *she* is to us.

Mate.

NERISSA

Three

"Pulling the wrong tail will get you bitten," Naia singsongs, her shoulder bumping mine before swimming past me and into my bedroom. She's been with me all night, making sure I don't get into trouble as any best friend should; the problem is, she's worse than I am.

Curious. Unafraid. Instigator extraordinaire, and the complete contradiction to every word of warning. She's been doing this all night, too. Ever since we snuck the rogues in, we used our siren's song to lull the wolfen patrol guards on the island's eastern side, then stayed to watch the uneven match.

Because I'd sent that rogue to his death. He *and* his friends, although the female remained semi-hesitant. She tried to fight back —run—but her brother was an accomplice and stood behind his idiot friend, Spiro.

It was easy. Almost too easy.

Lesson learned: Never steal from a mermaid.

We don't forgive. We don't forget.

And Spiro Marros's biggest mistake was breaking into my small home in Port Avaria, his grimy hands going through my jewelry. Mostly odds and ends, tide-hopper baubles of little to no value lost at sea that I've privately collected over the years without my king's knowledge. It's against mermaid law to do so; my grandfather would be pissed. He sees value in gold and silver—precious metals—but then again, I've never been one to walk a completely straight line.

More like a zigzag.

This is my rebellion.

Something that's just mine.

Marros paid the price for his greed, though. A sweet lullaby, a gentle command, and he walked into the wolf's den without a fight...

"You're stronger than him," I cooed, my voice thick with honeyed intent. I ran my pointer finger across his shoulder blades as I walked around him, my touch designed to further entice. Manipulate. "A real alpha—filthy pirate—wouldn't bow down to any man, much less rely on magic to keep his throne."

"He's unworthy," Spiro spit out, jaw tight, eyes full of malice as my will became his.

"Find the stone, rogue. Find it, and I'll reward you."

The glamour took root slowly, like poison ivy, and it threaded through the cracks his pride provided. I didn't push or yell, use the sharp edge of a shell to slash his face—I simply sang my request. Low and sweet, my words a pulse of magic thrumming beneath his skin.

"Remind them who you are, Marros," I purred, brushing aside particles of dirt from his shirt. "Make the wolves kneel."

His pupils dilated, and his breathing hitched. "I won't fail you, Princess Nerissa."

At that moment, he was nothing more than a puppet on a string.

And yet when faced against Alpha Daire, it was my enemy I... cheered for.

"There's just something about him," I mutter under my breath, turning away from Naia. She knows me too well. I can't and won't acknowledge whatever this pull is. From utter hatred to desire, and I want more.

Of him. Of the raw, animalistic power that exudes from his every pore.

Because there's no denying how ruggedly handsome Kai Daire is. Both beast and human.

He's tall, dark, and handsome with the blackest eyes that turn a warm, golden honey when the wolf comes to the forefront. Alpha Daire exudes power. It ripples off his tanned flesh in waves, while the tattoos decorating his back, arms, and neck only add to the allure.

Bones. Claws. A compass.

Each artful piece was chosen with care, executed with precision, and the result is a story etched in flesh. One I want to read. Memorize. Just once.

He's the perfect male specimen. A werewolf. *The enemy, Nerissa. Never forget that.*

"War and revenge don't follow the rules, Naia. Neither do I." Swimming toward the large window, I stare out onto the Marivelle kingdom below. Most houses are asleep, but a few early risers drift through the coral-lined streets. They're opening shops, harvesting sea herbs, and preparing for the change in tides.

Then, there's the switch of patrol on duty.

The brine-steel shoulder guard—a mix of crystalized salt deposits and abyssal brine pools—catches the streams of light, reflecting a myriad of colors, while the luminis kelp sash crosses their chest and weaves through a thick belt of the same material. Each member of the royal army serves two monthly patrol rotations in twelve-hour shifts, between training and other duties.

Their title, ranks, and names are engraved on the right arm guard, while the left holds our kingdom's crest forged in a bioluminescent ink mixture.

"Are you, Rissa? Having fun, that is?" she asks, gliding up next to me to watch the sun rise higher, reflecting over our water kingdom from the surface. It's early, and we haven't slept. I'm exhausted and confused. *Exhilarated.* "Because from where I'm floating, that wasn't innocent or—"

"I enjoyed myself." My tone comes out harsher than intended, but my need for her to drop it far exceeds her penchant to be nosy. Do I love her and the inherent way she can read me like an open book? Yes. Absolutely. Outside of my immediate family, she's the person I trust most.

Her loyalty to the crown is unfaltering. Her love for my grandmother is honest and pure.

She's my person. My chosen sister.

"Or you enjoyed the sweaty, muscle-glistening-under-the-moonlight wolf?" Naia's shoulder bumps mine, her lips curved in a salacious grin when I turn to look at her. No judgement or reproach. "I'm not blaming you, Nerissa. That man is gorgeous, even if he's the descendant of a rotten beast."

"Drop it," I grit out, not liking her admiration for his body or the insult. Neither sits well with me.

"That wasn't a no." *No. It wasn't.* "Will his looks prevent you from…" she trails off, but the implications are there.

What needs to be done goes beyond reclaiming the stone and returning it to its rightful place around my grandmother's neck. And yet, I can't control how my core clenches at the memory of him playing with his prey. The raw, animalistic strength behind each strike and the flush of want they caused; I felt the heat from my cheeks to my nipples. The tingle of awareness and desire.

I've never experienced goosebumps before, but I'm an expert in them now.

Every time he searched the open water for me, I bit back a whimper. Shivered when Kai Daire recognized my scent, focused, and forgot everything but the perfume carried over to him by a soft breeze.

Not Naia's. Not other wolves. *Me.*

"I need to see him again."

"What was that?" Naia asks, her brow arched. We both know she heard; she just wants me to say it out loud. "Come on. Say it."

"I need to see him again."

"And why is that?" Again, no reproach. If anything, I detect a hint of worry for me.

"Because this will all end on my terms." Not a lie. My grandfather's plan and mine differ. "It's my fate."

"Nerissa, I'm just—"

"Let's get some sleep before I'm summoned by our king," I say, cutting her off. "I'm exhausted."

Not a lie, and yet not the whole truth either. My body wants the rest, but my mind is awake. Too aware.

"Sure." Naia exhales roughly and extends her arms up and back, stretching her limbs. She doesn't push or call me out right now. Instead, she turns and heads toward the exit, but pauses at the threshold. "Lunch today?"

I shake my head when she looks at me from over her shoulder. "Can't. I've got something to take care of in Avaria."

"Want some company?"

"Not today."

"Then I'll run interception with your grandfather." A devilish smirk curls on her lips. "I'm sure His Majesty will be interested to learn about the problems young merwomen face. We can begin with the growing pressure to accept arranged marriages versus fated mates."

I snort. "Oh, he'd be thrilled at that."

My grandfather was a patriarch. At times sexist.

He believed a man should rule the siren kingdom, even though a woman was better equipped. Sure, my grandmother held power and her opinions were valued, but at the end of the day, her observations became his to take credit for. It was his protection and love that allowed her to be so *free*.

That wasn't freedom. It was chains disguised as jewelry, and I wasn't going to end up like her.

I played my part, did my duty as heir, but my position was clear to all:

No marriage agreement, unless it's to my fated mate.

"Right? Our king is always so worried about his constituents." The smile on her face drops then, her expression now serious. "Be careful, Nerissa. Come home safely. You're needed here."

"I promise."

THICK CORDED MUSCLES ripple with every movement while beads of sweat slide down his tanned skin. He's gorgeous, every inch of him attuned to my need as he picks me up and flips me into position.

I'm on all fours. My head is low and ass high.

Every inch of me is on display as I revel in his strength. In how easily he manhandles me.

But then again, I crave his control. Need his bite.

"Such a perfect little mate." Lips trace from the base of my neck to my shoulder, his canines nipping the skin along the way. A bite of pain before a touch of pleasure. "Are you ready for me, Princess?"

"Oh, Gods," I moan, clenching hard at the feel of his teeth. My hips push back against his thick length, silently begging him to take the gift I've saved for him. "Please."

"Not Gods, Nerissa. I'm your beast."

"Mine. Only mine." Low; it leaves me on a needy whine, and he chuckles above me. That laugh turns into a hiss, though, a rough curse as the thick head of his cock notches at my entrance.

It feels so good. So right.

"No man or wolf will ever love you more." His hips snap forward—

"Oh, fuck me," I gasp, sitting up in my bed. Chest heaving and inner thighs slick; I'm in my human form. *What the...* Two legs are lying on my clamshell bed, not my tail. I'm naked, and my body feels sensitive as if he'd touched me. As if it hadn't all been a dream, and I have no way to explain or justify the tingling pulse of need causing me to clench.

To moan low as a shiver runs through me; I feel exposed.

Mermaids rarely shift in water. We stay in our true form. Our tails are a special part of who we are, and mine holds more than just its beautiful, iridescent colors.

My birthmark is distinct and special; I carry the mark of dual moons.

My grandmother carries the same mark, while my mother didn't. Just as I have an affinity—my emotions are tied to the weather—and my mother had no ability. It skipped a generation.

Something that's never happened before, and while alive, my mother saw it as a blessing. She wasn't tied to serve the crown and preferred to stand down after finding her mate, letting my grandfather continue to lead. My father had no desire to be king, still doesn't, and I don't blame him.

Our kingdom isn't as free as tide-hoppers might think.

We're led by hierarchy and archaic roles where males have more power, and even though my grandmother was the true heir, her arranged mating took the crown. Unfair and wrong—I won't make the same mistake.

Closing my eyes and taking in a deep breath, I try to calm my racing heart. Attempt to slip back into my tail form, and yet, I fail. Over and over. My mind refuses to unsee those vibrant honeyed eyes and the way his head snapped in my direction; his jaw clenched tight as my scent swirled around him.

I'd played my hand last night.

A part of me wanted Kai to know I was there, even if I didn't show my face. One of the advantages of being Lucienne's granddaughter is the treasures she's handed down to me over the years. Ancient scriptures, an amulet hidden inside a gemstone bracelet that dulls my scent, a sea-silk woven cloak, the latter of which is my most coveted possession.

Its fibers shift to match any surroundings, working on both land

and sea while blending me into the background if need be. These were things she once used to escape and breathe away from *her* father's controlling grip.

Family. Duty. Sacrifice.

And yet you almost exposed yourself...

The breeze and storm last night weren't nature-born, but a mix of my emotions as I watched the powerful display. I couldn't help the fight within, how my body thrummed beneath the waist-deep water as he exerted his alpha's aura onto the crowd of bloodthirsty wolves.

It was sexy. It was a revelation.

It's haunting my dreams.

This is all his fault. Handsome asshole.

"What's wrong with me?" I groan out loud, throwing myself back, arm across my face. "Kai Daire is the enemy."

I'm frustrated and confused. Need to get control of myself.

Focusing on my breathing, I try to calm the upheaval that filthy wolf wrought upon me. I'm home, safe, and the soothing flow of the water begins to loosen the knot in my chest with each deep inhale. The more I give in to the slow rocking, the easier it is to calm down and not think of him.

His handsome face recedes, and instead, I picture myself taking a deep-sea swim.

Instead of his muscles and that woodsy scent I've barely uncovered, I'm brought to an image of myself sitting inside my home in Avaria, reading a book. Maybe sharing a meal with the older mage that lives next door that I've struck an unconventional friendship with.

"Did tell Naia I'd be busy." Originally, I was going to Avaria to ask some questions, but the idea of a private tarot reading tugs at me instead. It's quieter, more precise, and no one will ask questions back. Exhaling sharply, I push upright and smile. My tail shimmers back into existence, the purples and blues with a touch of soft pink catch the sunlight filtering down through the overhead openings.

More so when I drift toward the largest window and peer below.

The entire kingdom is awake and moving. The shops are open, their fronts bright with shells and abalone. Tiny merkids dart and laugh through the coral maze garden while a band sets up in the square, the running of instruments carrying through the current.

Signs of life are everywhere.

It all brings a smile to my face, until the scent of sea salt pauses outside my bedroom. Two men I know carry that same scent, a slight variation in each.

One is my grandfather. One is his godson, General Orion.

There's a pause there and a muttered—too low—exchange, but I'm able to make out two words clearly:

Cordis Lux.

One minute, there had been the flash of metal, the high arch of an arm aiming to kill, and then a half-shifted alpha, claws digging into the neck of the man I'd sent to investigate. Spiro's job was simple, and I'd stared at the rewards of my deception hanging from a thick gold chain, the black stone radiant under the moon's light...

That priceless gem belongs to my family. It was meant to be mine on the day I reached my eighteen summers, just like it had been for every daughter before me. In each generation, one girl is born—a gift from the gods—and she carries abilities her brothers will never inherit.

It's always been this way.

I was robbed of this rite of passage, and at twenty-one now, it still burns.

The stone is passed down my grandmother's side of the family. Presented through a binding ritual, it carries a piece of our magic we'd one day gift our fated one. A blessing meant to strengthen and protect, mark them as ours.

Possessive: it's our scent that intertwines with the very fibers of their DNA.

Obsidian, black and smooth like sea glass, it remains dormant until touched by fate. Glowing a fiery blue only when true mates touch and the bond snaps into place. Moreover, after the bite, it's tradition for the male to keep it close to his chest until their daughter comes of age, and then it's passed down.

That tradition died with the betrayal of Queen Lucienne, though.

It's made her weak. Sick. *Lost.*

My grandmother hasn't been the same since Ephraim Daire stole it from her, and that's a wrong I've vowed to right, no matter the cost. Even if it means killing the king of all wolves and displaying his black, pirate heart at the entrance to the Marivelle kingdom, so be it.

Family comes first. No matter the cost.

But what if I'm the price?

NERISSA

Four

"Lost in thought, Princess?" I'm pulled back to the present by a sudden, gruff voice, and my body turns to face the intruder. Smile a little cocky, Orion stands closer than I expected. A few feet from me, he has broad shoulders, average height, and a dark blue tail that matches his eyes. In contrast, his hair is white—almost silver—beneath the sun's rays. "What's got you so preoccupied?"

His eyes traverse my body, up and down from my fin to my breasts. They're covered in my favorite kelp silk bra with shell accents polished to look like glass beads in shades that match my tail. Orion doesn't hide his attraction, and I'm uncomfortable, but that's nothing new. It's been the same since we were young.

Back then, it was his pompous attitude.

Now, he's overconfident and pushy. Forgets that in the hierarchy, he's below me.

He's the son of Grandfather Atlas's friend, groomed from a young age to be our general after his father stepped down. Not that he fought for or earned the position; his reward came simply from being the son of a loyal advisor and court member. The same man who stepped in when my grandfather became king, personally chosen for that position.

"Morning," I say, my voice low as I glide backwards, a practiced smile in place.

"It's past noon, Nerissa. Way past morning."

"I just woke up, so for me..." I trail off, the meaning clear.

"Would it make you happy if I said it?" In response, I arch a brow but remain quiet. Orion exhales roughly at that, the scales along his chest vibrating. "Good morning, Your Majesty."

"Was that so hard?" I ask, but before he can reply, I continue. "And to answer your earlier question, I'm thinking—"

"About?" I don't call out his rudeness for cutting me off. Instead, I swim around him toward the entryway. I've never liked being alone with him. *Opportunist and a chauvinist.* "Where are you going?"

Pausing at the entryway, I look back at him from over my shoulder. "Is that truly any of your business?"

"I'm not the enemy."

"Yet, you're delaying my trip to the kitchen."

"No one told you to sleep in."

"Is that an admonishment I detect?" My tone is a little sharp, but like everything else, it goes right over his head.

"Where were you last night?"

"You're overstepping, General. Remember your place."

His shitty grin says he enjoys my annoyance. "Be nice."

"Orion, I'm five seconds from—"

"Your grandfather requests your presence in the dining hall, Nerissa." He swims toward me, skimming his arm against my side before stopping outside my room. There, he waves a hand toward the royal feast chambers. Without a word, I move to pass by him, but his hand shoots out and takes hold of my wrist. Shuddering is my immediate response, but I fight the urge back and stare at his hand on mine. "I picked up your favorite moon leaf cakes with sea grapes."

My favorite? Yes.

Do I trust him? No.

"Thank you, General."

"It's my pleasure."

He moves closer, but I shake my head. "Now let go."

"Of course." A squeeze to my fingers, and he lets go. I swim away, ignoring the way his shadow clings to me. Orion follows me from my private quarters to the dining hall, my stomach twisting with hunger and trepidation. *Why does Grandfather want to see me?*

"Let me get the door for you."

There isn't a door, but I don't call him out on it. The thick, beaded curtain hangs from the opening to the floor with its opaque white glass, creating a subtle song. Each shift in the current brings a different set of notes, but they combine into my grandmother's favorite song.

A land-born one. From Avaria.

I'm the only one who knows this, and I can't help the small smile that tugs at my lips as it plays. It's sweet yet haunting; a melody full of want and need that's unreciprocated—of what ifs.

I slip into the room, careful not to let the swish of my tail echo too loudly. Don't thank Orion, either, and stop beside my grandfather, who's already at the head of the table. This dining room is private. Meant to give the royals a sense of normalcy and share a meal, but it's always felt like a strategy meeting rather than downtime.

Grandfather's eyes snap to me, sharp as a blade, before softening. "Nerissa, my child. How are you?"

He doesn't look a day over forty for a merman over a hundred years old. We age slowly. Mermen carry their years gently, time passing by us like a current, leaving faint traces on our faces while never stealing our beauty.

Bending a bit, I kiss my grandfather's cheek before placing my forehead against his. We stay like that for a few seconds, a recognition of our familial bond and love—even if at times, I don't like the man. The things he does. He's charming when it's to his benefit, demanding of his subjects, and the biggest advocate for a patriarchal society where merwomen live beneath the forced protection of the crown and their king.

Is he also loving to those he cares about? Yes.

Is he faithful to my grandmother and our queen? Yes.

Is he open-minded or believes in change? No. Absolutely not.

He's kept the crown by luck and my mother finding her true mate, the son of a chancellor from the western sea; he moved here from a smaller pod in the Sea of Eternal Night with no delusions of grandeur or ulterior motives, yet loyal to their king. My father has no desire to rule; he simply loved my mother until she took her last breath, the end of a harpoon embedded deep in her chest.

I was only two years old at the time.

"Everything okay?"

His question brings me back to the present, and I smile. Nodding. "I'm well, just a bit famished."

"You got in late?" This time, it's not a question but a direct observation. One that needs a response he won't dig too deep into. "One would say early morning, to be exact."

"I did, but with good reason." He waves me forward to take a seat, and I'm left with no choice but to accept the chair pulled back by Orion. "Thank you."

"My pleasure, Princess." Grandfather smiles at the display with fondness in his eyes, a clear desire for me to accept this match. One he's mentioned in passing before, but I worry the time for a more direct command is coming. To him, a mate is a compromise between two people who find gain through the union.

Me? I'll only accept a fated match. My soulmate.

"It's good to see you two getting along."

"Why wouldn't we?" I ask, picking up one of the sea grapes and popping it into my mouth. The skin bursts beneath my teeth, sweet and tart all at once, like a ripened plum kissed by salt. They're tiny, but their taste lingers on my tongue, and I can't help the honest grin that stretches across my lips.

I'm reminded of afternoons with my father after a fighting lesson; he always brought some as a reward.

"Of course, you would." Grandfather's hand pats my arm, his tone indulgent. "But I'm still curious about your whereabouts last night, Nerissa. Where were you?"

"I might've done some recon work last night."

"And did you find anything?" My nod has him exhaling roughly, his scales vibrating along his arms and chest. "Where? What did you see?"

"I followed a pirate ship—"

"By yourself," he thunders, his hand slamming atop the carved coral table. A crack forms, and Orion shifts closer, but my grandfather turns his head and stares him down. His general falls back immediately, his head lower, but I still catch the way his hand clenches when our king turns back to me. "Answer me, Nerissa. Who gave you permission to get close to those filthy mutts?"

"Did you or did you not want me to find it?"

"Yes, but—"

"I saw it." Immediately, pride dances across his features, but I catch the undercurrent of calculation beneath it. "He has it."

"Are you sure you saw it?" It says a lot that he didn't reprimand me for cutting him off a few seconds ago. "Who has it now?"

"Yes." Behind my eyes, I see it again. Alpha Kai Daire. The stone around his neck. Those blazing eyes looking out toward the sea, unable to find me. "It called to me yesterday, this unexplainable pull, and I followed my gut. They were on the Isle of San Tico—"

"Who wore it?"

"Kai Daire."

"Where?"

"On a chain." Do I omit mesmerizing the rogue and sending him in on purpose? Yes. The less he knows, the better. "But I left before any wolf could pick up my scent."

"You've done well, my child." His once tense fingers start drumming on the table. There's no anger on his face, but more of a calculated expression. "You've surpassed my expectations. You notice things others don't, more so than your grandmother." For a second, I feel a sharp pang of pain in my chest, and I know it's his. Why he's projecting, I don't know, but it runs deep. As king, he has the ability to absorb and exude emotions. To help his subjects when in distress, but right now, I feel him. "She's getting weaker, Nerissa. Every day she's without that stone—the magic stolen—her soul and body wither. I'm worried about her."

"I am too."

"Blessed be the gods who illuminated your way."

"We need it back before it's too—"

"Already harassing my daughter, Atlas?" Orion bristles at my father's lack of proper address, but knows his place and stays quiet. Or it could be jealousy. While he's reminded not to step out of line, we don't adhere to the same rules. Dad heads toward me then, stopping to kiss my forehead before swiping one of my cakes. He pops it into his mouth, sending me a wink before I can complain. "At least let her eat before the interrogation."

Grandfather's in such a good mood now that he pushes the plate closer to me. "My apologies, sweetheart. Please eat."

"Thank you." Picking up a piece, I chew slowly, savoring the rich balance between salty and sweet. It's a perfect consistency, not too moist, even though we're underwater and its exposure should ruin the pastry. The cream filling is a mix of seafoam and sea grapes, giving it a gentle, lingering sweetness with a kiss of salt. Then, there's the delicate shell leaf wrap holding it together. It's soft yet resilient, and a favorite of mermaids.

"Your grandmother's waiting for you," Dad says after I've eaten two palm-sized cakes. I'm already pushing back before he can finish, rushing to give a quick bow and grab the plate as I head out of the room. All I catch at the end is, "…sitting room."

ALPHA
KAI

FIVE

"She was here," I say, staring out at the crashing tide. It's bright out, the sun high overhead, and I watch the wolfen pack ships become smaller with each passing minute. The island's empty now; all attending leaders and their vessels are gone, including my pack members and new prisoners.

I couldn't leave, though. Not when there's a small possibility that *she* could return.

My wolf is restless. A little angry.

He's fighting against my tight hold—wants to tear free and find the owner of that decadent scent:

Orange blossoms and coconut, edged with sweet vanilla.

Unique. Enticing. Mouth-watering.

We'll find her, I console him, but the rumble that builds inside my chest and slips through my lips is not one of appeasement. It's a demand, and I nod, promising to hunt her down. That scent is woven into my genetic makeup, impossible to forget, and there's nowhere in this world she can hide from me. *Could she be…?*

A warm breeze drifts across my bare chest, and I smell the traces of blood and salt dried on my skin. It disrupts my thoughts, but this time, the scent is different. Familiar, but not the one I want.

"I thought you might want some company, Son," my father says from behind me as we overlook the ocean from a small cliff. It's close to where I'd seen her silhouette pass, one I need to appear again. He takes a seat beside me on a weather-worn stone over-looking the beach and passes a black-labeled bottle of rum, which I take. "What's bothering you?"

"I scented her."

He doesn't ask me who *she* is, just nods. "Are you sure, Kai?"

"Orange blossoms, coconut, and vanilla." Holding the rum out to him, I wait for my father to tap his half-empty bottle with mine before taking a deep pull. The spirit is spiced yet smooth, warming my chest before settling into a nice tingling buzz that spreads through my limbs.

"Ahhh." His smile and the glassy look in his eyes are ones I ignore, especially knowing it's my mother he's thinking of. Julius Daire, our past alpha, is known for his temper and bloodthirst—he ruled with an iron fist, yet for his mate, he's a docile pup. Never understood it, but I never questioned it either. "You'll never forget the moment you scented your mate."

"It happened during my challenge."

At that, he snorts and takes another sip. Then two more swallows of the amber rum. "Poor girl. Where are you hiding her?"

"She disappeared."

His brows furrow, and all earlier amusement is now gone. "What do you mean, she's gone?

I don't answer him right away. Instead, I exhale roughly and scratch my short beard. It's been a few days since I trimmed it, and it's now the perfect length to tug. And I do, the small bite of pain clearing my head while a few more sips of rum feel appropriate.

Celebratory.

For a few minutes, we sit like this. Above us, birds fly while small waves crash on the shore, the horizon vast and never-ending. But more than that, his silence is like a mirror—

Steady. Measured. *Understanding.*

Mates are sacred. There's nothing a wolf won't do to find and claim their goddess-given gift, and for an alpha, the compulsion is near overwhelming. A dominant force that drives until the need is met.

For companionship. For a family.

"Did it...?" Dad says, breaking the silence. His eyes are on the stone around my neck, so much knowledge in his dark eyes, their color the same shade as mine.

"For a moment." Lifting my unoccupied hand to my chain, I enclose the black gem in my palm. It's cold. Its weight is a constant reminder of what *she* could be. "When her scent hit me, I felt it grow warm, but then—"

"Then?"

"Nothing." Craning my neck from side to side, I stretch the tight, sore muscles there. Feel the pop of a few places that had been pinched tight; the relief is instantaneous. "It grew cold, and I blinked. Somehow, between the two actions, she disappeared."

He leans forward, resting his elbows on his knees. What's left of his liquor is dangling from his fingertips. "And your wolf? His reaction?"

"He's unsettled. Wants to hunt."

"Not surprising." Dad grins at me, his expression more than amusement. He's enjoying this. "So what are you going to do now?"

"What do you think?" The look I shoot him is incredulous, while a warning growl slips through clenched teeth. "I'm not letting this go."

"I'll drink to that." Lifting the bottle to his lips, he tips it back and empties what's left. The glass falls with a dull thud on the ground, rolling right over the edge and onto the rocks below. It shatters upon impact, which he shrugs at.

"I'm not taking you home."

"Welcome to hell," we say in unison, but his words are a little slurred now. His slap on my back lands just as hard. Not that it'll last long. Our metabolism will burn through the alcohol fast. Still amusing, though. "The real alpha's challenge just started."

"I know." Taking a page out of his book, I knock back what's left of my bottle in one continuous pull. I don't stop until it's empty, and my chest rumbles with my wolf's agreement. *The way her scent calls to me can't be a one-off.* "I'll chase her to the end of the fucking world if I have to."

NERISSA

Six

"**C**ome in, Love." Grandmother Lucienne's whisper reaches me seconds before I enter the room. Her voice is soft, yet the exhaustion is clear. Heavy. It's only because of our keen sense of hearing that I'm able to discern what she says, just as she's aware of my presence because of the same.

We sense movement and noise, sensitive to the most minute change.

"You called for me, Gran?" I stop next to her chair and place my forehead against hers. For a moment, we exchange warmth—the tethers of our auras embracing as they recognize each other for what we are. Family: we're tied together by love and blood. And while I do the same with other members of my family or close friends, with her, it's different. More. The matching birthmarks on our tails, the dual moons, have intertwined our fates since before my birth.

You don't put demands on fate. You follow and trust.

I've heard that saying all my life.

From her. From my father.

And I've been patient, but when I pull back and meet her eyes again, there's a warning in there…

"I did, young one." Grandma coughs, the sound faint, but then she clicks her tongue. Fast and sharp, a trilling sound—my brows furrow. "Ignore that."

"Not possible." Tilting my head to the side, I study her. "What's going on?"

"I'm worried." Her small fingers intertwine with mine. They squeeze, but there's no true strength behind it.

"About? Why are you—"

"Please sit, Nerissa." A command, one I adhere to out of respect *and* surprise. She's not one to do so, but more than that, this moment feels off.

As if I'm missing something.

Taking a seat, I scan the room but find nothing out of order.

The queen's sitting room is carved from pale limestone, smoothed by centuries of water and gleaming with veins of pearl that catch the filtered light. Heavy thrones of reef and obsidian anchor the space, their seats softened by anemone-woven pads and sea sponge padding, their fibers swaying faintly in the water. Shell inlaid tables shine, their surfaces etched with swirling designs, while kelp drapes give the room a cozy, private feel.

"You're not going to find what you're looking for here."

"I'm not—"

"Don't lie to me," she says, her tone admonishing yet soft. "You're playing a dangerous game, sweetheart. One I beg you to stop."

"I don't understand what you mean."

"Alpha Kai Daire." Those three words stop me cold, but the way she says his last name sends a ripple of awareness through me. It's not disgust I detect, but…*sadness*. "Whatever you think you know—"

"Everything I do is for the good of our kingdom."

Her exhale is full of reproach. A little disappointment. "Your heart might be in the right place, my child, but this is not your fight."

"Grandma, I don't understand." A tiny bit of hurt slips through my tone, but I'm also curious. Her eyes are begging me to let this go. To trust her. "What aren't you telling me?"

"That you're wrong, Nerissa. Please. Leave it alone." Her gaze sharpens, voice dropping low. It stings to be on the receiving end of her disappointment—I don't understand *why*—but she reaches a hand out to me, palm up. I place mine atop hers, and there's a subtle vibration between our skin, like a thrumming pulse, and it reminds me of the way our scales shake depending on our emotions. "I'm asking you to stop hunting whatever your grandfather has you chasing before the cost and repercussions are more than you're willing to pay."

"Grandma, I need more than that. What aren't you telling me?"

"You don't put demands on fate…"

"You follow and trust," I finish for her, then exhale slowly. For a minute or two, we don't speak. The waters are calm, and yet I feel the shift of movement not far from us. She does, too.

Grandma lowers her head, and I meet her halfway. Our heads are close, her lips now pressed against my temple. "I need you to go to Avaria, Nerissa. Today."

"I'm actually heading there—"

"I know." The presence draws nearer, and we exhale in relief when we catch my father's scent. He doesn't come in, but lingers as if protecting the area. "There's something I need you to retrieve for me. It's important, but more than that, I need you to be discreet. No one can know."

I'm nodding before she's done. "Understood."

"Your neighbor has a note from me."

"Instructions?"

"In a sense…" A small knock just outside the door causes Grandma to trail off, but then Dad pokes his head in. He's smiling at us. "Everything okay, Marin?"

"We have eyes."

"Are you two sneaking me out?" It'd be comical, if not for the disgust on my father's face. There's also a low rumble bordering on a warning sound. Mermen and merwomen don't growl like tide-hoppers; ours is more of a hum. A deep bass vibration that cuts through the water, slicing across the gills and attacking the nervous system.

You're thrown off if not prepared. More so if it comes from a high-ranking member of the kingdom.

"Orion's showing his hand."

"Meaning?" I ask my father, eyes on him, but I don't miss the look they share.

"Meaning it's getting late, Princess. Go have some fun."

THE WARM, late-afternoon sun feels good on my skin, but it's the salty breeze that soothes me as I break through the surface. It carries a touch of wet earth from an earlier rain and the ocean's natural essence, a combination that brings me peace the closer to land I get.

There's a sense of *home* I don't understand, yet I don't shy away from either. Instead, I close my eyes and take in another deep inhale while blindly pulling back the hood.

There's still so much going through my head, a myriad of frag-mented conversations—the memory of that Alpha Kai searching the shoreline for my scent—but my Grandmother's words are the loud-est. They demand my compliance. My complete obedience.

Stop hunting whatever your grandfather has you chasing before the cost and repercussions are more than you're willing to pay.

She repeated those words right before I left with my father, taking a private exit that no one outside of the family knows exists. My great-grandfather made the addition, a way for his wife and child to escape if the need ever arose, and today it came in handy.

With a kiss to her cheek, I swam out with Dad, parting ways after exiting the castle. His expression held a tenderness that I haven't seen in a while, not that the man hasn't been the most amazing parent, but it was... different.

Wistful.

He hugged me tight before letting go. His words were low. "Follow your heart, Nerissa."

The streets were still busy then, and with the change in tides coming in soon, people were rushing about. It was easy to mix in, going unnoticed as the cloak kept my scent and aura hidden.

Within minutes, I was far enough to slip behind a grouping of tall pillars and swim toward Avaria.

"Why doesn't she want her magic back?" I ask aloud, my body shifting into my human skin. Curves replace my fins, wide hips giving way to long, lithe legs, and toes painted in the same varying shades as my tail. Scales recede, leaving tan skin behind—soft and glowing, kissed by a fine mist of water that clings to every mermaid ashore. It's unnoticeable to most, but for those who know, it's our one tell.

The first step onto land is always strange. Warm grains press beneath my toes, unfamiliar yet grounding in a way that's soothing.

I stretch my neck from side to side, loosening the pull of trans-formation while a few strands of wet hair cling to my face. Light slams into me, and it's harsh for a moment—too bright after the blue depths—and for a second, the world blurs. It's gone within a few blinks; shapes sharpen, and the jagged coastline comes into focus.

The beach is empty, but not the port. I'm close enough to see, but not be seen, even without the cloak, and I make out three ships docked while another gets closer. The latter is larger. Its sails are dark, but not black.

A sliver of disappointment courses through me.

"Get it together, Nerissa. Enough already," I mutter under my breath. My cloak covers me, and I pull the hood up, walking up the beach and toward the small coastal town where I own a home. It's small compared to anything my family owns in our kingdom, but it's mine.

No family. No rules. No set expectations from anyone.

Most of the people who reside in Avaria are merchants: a mix of witches, wolves, and one dragon clan that manages the port for the royal wolf pack. It's a mutually beneficial contract, making them a tax-free business while the pirates collect—get information on who docks here and why.

Then, there are the hybrids. Or day walkers, as locals call them.

They're the offspring of both a female fae and a male vampire—a union that should never exist. Cursed to crave blood but still roam the light. They feed on the essence of the donor, not just their blood. A trade that satisfies both, their pleasure sealed through satiated moans.

It's not far from Isla de Lobos, where the werewolf monarch pack resides, or so they call themselves now. A century ago, they were nothing but filthy, greedy pirates.

Ruthless. Pillaging. Feral.

The open waters are their playground, a vast oasis with no rules used to steal and conquer—the merpeople never intervened. We didn't care about the disputes of savages or the clash of shifters and other magic-wielding beings until they touched our sacred stone.

Used my grandmother's magic.

And yet you still find that brutal beast handsome?

Can't deny it, either. Have for a while now.

Much longer than anyone, even my best friend, knows.

I'm intrigued by the animal—want more of a man I've been taught to hate—even if all it can ever be is a one-time encounter. Because there's something delicious about the forbidden, and Kai Daire is just that.

Taboo. Deadly. Beautiful.

To want him is treason. To crave his touch is a curse.

And yet you want a taste.

That wolf is an enemy to the merpeople's crown: a direct descendant of the man who stole my grandmother's magic and Cordis Lux stone, leaving her with a broken promise and vulnerable to attacks, something I could never forgive.

She's in danger because of Ephraim Daire.

I can't forget that.

My nose twitches then; a sharp note rides the cool breeze, pulling me from my thoughts.

Without consent, my steps slow as I pass a small inn, its faded wood and bougainvillea-framed windows catching the sunlight. The vines are lush and the flowers bright while a new scent curls around me…

Guaiac wood, smoky and deep, wrapped within the sweetness of pineapple. There's also something deeper beneath it. Darker. The faint, almost whisper of leather, feels like a vine shackling me to the present.

My chest tightens.

It's familiar yet strange, like a memory I didn't know I had.

My fangs ache. My body thrums with renewed excitement.

Gods help me, I want more of that scent.

"I need to find it."

ALPHA KAI

SEVEN

My boots are heavy as they strike the damp dock, the sharp sound cracking through the hectic, late afternoon noise of Port Avaria. The wood vibrates beneath my weight, each step louder than the last as those around me stop and give a respectful nod of acknowledgement.

This territory is under my control. Protection.

Men part without being told, while the few women offering a warm welcome to sailors pause mid-step. Yet it's the following bout of silence that almost pulls a smile from my face. *Almost.*

I'm too restless. Have been for the last few days.

That fucking scent.

It haunts me. Can almost taste it in the air at every turn.

Need to find the owner. The stone will tell me.

Eyes track my movement, and I can feel it—the shift in the air as I make my way to the end of the pier. Behind me, large ships unload merchandise while others pick up deckhands to help transport goods. I don't involve myself with their affairs; they pay for my protection, and I keep it transactional unless someone is greedy enough to involve vampires.

I take those vile creatures being anywhere near my property as an insult. Just as I do sirens.

Don't trust them. Never will.

Been a while since we destroyed one of their transport ships.

My wolf stretches under my skin at the thought, his claws raking my insides, and I make a mental note to come back and inspect the dock's logs. A dragon elder steps forward then, a bag in his hand, but I shake my head. Not now. I'll be back to speak with him and collect, but I have somewhere to be first.

"I'll be here when you're ready, Alpha Kai," he says, his scales glimmering under his skin. He's already stepping away while I acknowledge his attention with a firm nod. Nothing else.

I've got no time to waste, leaving behind a few of my crew members, my Gamma among them, to keep the ship ready to set sail. He'll keep them in line, eyes sharp while protecting the treasure I've left inside my private quarters.

The Cordis Lux. A siren's gift to appease her guilt and betrayal.

I'm heading toward the center of town where the local inn and blacksmith have businesses close to each other. The owners, a husband and wife pair of omega wolves from my pack, keep an eye on things for me. That, and he does flawless work with weaponry. He's the only one I trust to service my swords.

The closer to the town's center I get, the louder the buzz of merchants and residents becomes. A few witches turn toward me and then look away. Another young female, a fae I've never seen before, rushes off in the direction of the textile shop.

I ignore them all, continuing toward the blacksmith. And the closer I get, the more on edge my wolf becomes. Pushing. A low, warning growl builds in my chest, and those around me take heed to the sound, slipping inside their homes and businesses as I walk down the street.

Stand down, I grit out when my fangs drop, piercing my bottom lip while claws rip through the nail beds. My pace picks up. My chest begins to expand with each deep inhale...

"Motherfuck," I grit out through clenched teeth, my muscles locking into place as *that* scent hits me once again. Floral and sweet. Bright orange blossoms, warm coconut, and the finest edge of vanilla round out the notes. It spears straight into me, pulling an answering rumble from my wolf.

He wants out. To hunt for the owner of this decadent perfume.

Because it's the same one from a few nights ago on Isla San Tico during the challenges. Beneath the blood and stench of rogues, I'd caught it—savored it on my tongue while the notes branded itself into my DNA.

I've thought about it. I want to hoard it.

Sunshine and sin.

Sweet enough to tempt and decadent enough to ruin.

She's here.

I'm not coming back tonight, I mindlink Torren, and it takes my gamma seconds to reply with his confirmation. No questions or need for instructions. He knows when to give me space.

Knows the difference between when I want company, and when man and beast want blood. Two sides of the same coin, and yet, I'm not myself today. Haven't been since I came across that sultry scent, the same one that causes me to turn left instead of right and head in the opposite direction of what I'd come to do.

I'm led toward a cliff where a small cropping of cottages sits. There are three of them, all about the same size, but I'm drawn to the one closest to the edge and with the clearest view of the active water below. It's quaint and painted a light blue with white shutters while the flowerbed blooms with varying plants and flowers.

Behind it, there's a thick jungle of tropical trees and native foliage untouched and respected by everyone on the island. Nothing is to be cut down or eradicated unless its use is medicinal or for sacred ceremonies held by the mages.

"Find her." Closing my eyes, I inhale deeply as the wolf comes forward. The change tears through me, spine arching as bones grind and stretch—cracking under the force of my beast's unleashing. Muscles swell, cords thickening and ripping through the fabric of my shirt and trousers as heat pours from my skin.

My clawed hands dig into the earth, skin splitting as my nails become black-tipped talons, and a snarl rips from my throat. Raw. Guttural. The sound carries, and in the distance, I hear the answering growls of my men aboard my ship. Not that I pay any mind to them or the mindlink from Torren asking me if everything is okay.

Man and beast are of a singular focus.

My jaw distends and teeth lengthen, aching with the need to bite through flesh while black fur spreads, not leaving a single inch of skin visible. The only contrast remains my wolf's honey-colored eyes and a line of pelt in the same shade down my spine.

A complete shift, I let my wolf form take complete control.

Shaking myself out, my nose flares, picking up notes of orange blossom and coconut. It's stronger—clearer in my animal form—and I memorize each one while prowling outside her home. I circle the property, rubbing my flanks along the walls and porch before licking a stripe across her front door. Predatory. Claiming.

Man and wolf are only satisfied when my scent marks the property, and only then do I release a deep and possessive howl. Approval and satisfaction resonate through the sound; my intent is clear to anyone who comes near the property, and the resident wolves of Avaria respond with a howl of their own.

It's loud, filling the town with our brethren's call, and yet I'm pulled away by the flutter of a warm breeze across my fur...

It's coming from the center of town. Her.

Lifting my snout high, I inhale deep before taking off. The heavy thud of my paws rattles the ground while my claws leave deep gouges in the ground. Grass and dirt, and then the solid cobblestone streets bear the aftermath of my haste—the weight of an alpha wolf mid hunt.

Nothing registers or matters but that seductive perfume and the hold it has on me.

For a shifter, the mate bond is sacred. A gift from the goddess herself to her children, two beings created from two halves of a soul, that only feel complete when reunited again. She doesn't make mistakes; each pairing is perfect and meant to bring joy and peace to each other.

You grow. You lean on.

You have a safe place to lay your head and loving arms that don't judge.

She has to be...

Most of the residents have vanished as I run down the street where the scent is strongest. The few outside are shop owners, mostly wolves themselves, and they bow their heads as I pass. No one speaks, but their submission is sharp and instinctive.

They know. Respect.

An alpha in the midst of a hunt doesn't stop until his prey is caught.

The wind picks up again, and this time, it feels as if it's curling a finger in front of my snout, taking me past my original destination. I pass a small herb shop, coffee shop, the inn, and the blacksmith—

A tavern sits at the end, two men standing outside, each holding a glass filled to the brim with beer. Its hoppy scent angers me, and I bare my teeth, a deep growl resonating from my chest. The two take a few steps back, never giving me their backs, and I stand guard outside the bar until they disappear around the corner.

Only then do I relax enough to retake the reins, my body shifting back into human form.

Fur becomes skin, and bones realign; my muzzle is now a sharp jaw. My fangs don't retract, though. Instead, they throb with an urgency I've never experienced before.

To bite. To be stained with her blood.

I'm walking toward the entrance, only pausing long enough to grab a pair of trousers from a communal box of unworn clothes kept throughout the town for shifters. They're on with the zipper half-closed within seconds, but then I'm shoving the door open.

The wood bangs against the opposite wall with a crack that silences the room. Multiple heads turn in my direction, but my warning growl has them looking away as my neck snaps to the right.

I find her automatically.

So pretty. So delicate.

My prey sits near the wall with the sweetest fucking face I've ever seen. Her lips are full and pouty, a soft shade of pink that contrasts perfectly with the delicate slope of her nose. But it's her eyes—violet, wide, and bright—that hold me captive. The shade is unique. Reminds me of something, but then my eyes shift, and I'm taken by a sea of black.

Dark waves frame her face, tumbling down her shoulders and back, and I find myself annoyed with the table keeping me from seeing where each strand ends. My hands clench, fingers twitching to touch the ends before I wrap them in a tight grip.

Lower, and I'm tracing the fragile line of her chin, then neck, pausing on her exposed collarbones. No bite. No claim.

A deep, guttural growl of approval leaves me then while she makes a low clicking noise. The sound is almost indiscernible, the kind one makes when something sour hits your tongue and your face scrunches up. Odd, and for a second my brows furrow, but then there's a subtle shift, pulling my attention toward the space beside her.

She isn't alone. There's a mage to her right, glasses low on her nose, and she whispers something I barely catch. All I can make out are the words *trust and lie* before she stands, tapping two fingers on the cover of an old book. Then the witch leaves, giving me a wide berth as she walks past me and out the door.

Most of the patrons do the same.

At this time of day, business hasn't picked up yet. The rowdier crowd arrives after the sun sets and animals want to play. Not all unmated shifters wait, and sex is a need they give in to.

But more than that, this temptress won't be here when they walk through those doors.

I don't share.

"Come with me, little treasure," I say, holding my hand out to her, palm facing up. The words are a little garbled as my wolf rises to the surface. I'm taking in every beautiful inch of her through my eyes, reveling in the way her scent curls around us like a sinful caress. But more than that, we know.

Werewolves are possessive creatures by nature, and jealousy is an unforgiving emotion. It dominates, making the calmest of men into feral beasts when challenged. When their mates are coveted.

And even without the stone, I do not doubt that she is mine.

NERISSA

Eight

This isn't good. Monumentally, a huge mistake.

For two days, I've wandered through town searching for the owner of the guaiac wood and pineapple combination. Its traces follow me, but there's no one there. Taunt me, and without conscious thought, I find myself walking in front of the wolf-owned inn and the blacksmith shop her husband owns.

I'm met with a dead end every single time, unable to answer what this could all mean.

The couple doesn't ask, but I sense their stares and lingering questions. My father's been sending me sonar pulses through the water just beyond my home, but I've asked him for more time. No explanation given, just a plea from his daughter.

Stupid? Maybe.

Irresponsible? Yes.

And yet, I didn't care until the moment Alpha Kai Daire walked through the tavern's door.

Imposing, his aura fills the room, and every head turns in his direction. There's a rumble in his chest, while large fangs peek through his lips, the latter of which are curled up in a snarl.

Dark, dangerous eyes meet mine. His attention is on me, and I feel the old mage beside me tense, what sounds like an *oh my* coming from her thin lips.

Not that I look away from the man. I can't.

More so when I'm slammed with the unique scent I've been desperate to find.

"This is bad," I mutter low, a sound that to a tide-hopper sounds like a series of clicks. He hears it, though, and I'm afraid to ask if he understands my language. Not that it matters a second later when those dark pools shift to the older woman beside me.

It's fleeting. Barely a few ticks of the clock, and yet, I don't like it.

Almost bristle in annoyance.

What the hell is wrong with me? I need to get out of here.

Magda clears her throat then, hand already reaching for her canvas bag. "I'll be leaving now."

"I'm not sure you—"

"Come find me tomorrow before you head home." With the tips of two fingers, she taps the book I'd been summoned to pick up. It's already protected, the preservation spell making it waterproof and only to be opened by the queen herself. "Truth and lies, my child. Hide one and expose the other."

Before I can ask what she meant, Magda is up and out of the tavern. Many others follow suit, and the ones who decide to stay keep a wide berth between themselves and the imposing alpha wolf. The same man who steps closer, his bare feet padding across the wooden floor until he's towering over my much smaller frame.

His expression is guarded, but there's something soft about his eyes. A warm mix of chocolate and honey, they fluctuate between the two shades, and there's no hiding the slight crinkles at the corner. *Smiling with his eyes.*

He's also bare-chested.

Strong and sinuous, his muscles bulge—the thick cords tensing while his nostrils flare. He's scenting me, and I follow the rapid rise and fall of his chest with rapt attention. Because he's a gorgeous man. No mistaking that.

Tall. Dark. Handsome.

Every solid inch of my enemy has been designed and carved by the goddess herself, a literal manifestation of all that I find attractive in a man. Easily over six foot five, if not taller, Alpha Daire makes me feel small. Tiny. Delicate against his sharp muscles—a jaw carved of stone—and I take him in as desperately as he does me.

My tanned skin prickles with awareness as his gaze travels lower; I do the same.

Tattoos. Dark ink against olive skin.

From the base of his neck down to his ribcage, ink marks his skin in brutal detail. Vertebrae stacked, ribs arcing outward, and every line and bone etched as though his skeleton had clawed its way outward. Black and gray shadows turn his body into a living X-ray, while on each wrist, there is the clear imprint of a black paw. *His wolf.*

I've heard of that before but never paid enough attention to the local wolves here. Or maybe it's just an alpha thing—the sign that its wolf has awakened and he or she is dominant.

They're stunning. Intricate yet intimidating, but it's the compass on his neck that draws my eye. The coordinates in it cause my brows to furrow, as if I should understand their meaning, but I'm pulled from the thought by a hand extending toward me, palm up.

Long, rough fingers. Hands that have labored and killed, if needed.

I've seen them bloody before. That night on the beach, even from afar, my keen eyesight didn't let me miss a single detail, and I craved for those blood-soaked claws to trace the length of my spine before gripping me—

"Come with me, little treasure," he says, and the deep tones resonate with a hidden place inside of me. It's rough, the animal there and commanding, and I find myself placing my hand atop his without conscious thought. The compulsion to be closer is undeniable, and I'm lost to the small curve of his lip when our skin touches.

What is that?

Tiny electrical pulses dance across my palm; they extend from the tip of my fingers, crawling up my wrist and arm. It almost tickles. The small bursts of playful energy dart between our hands, anchoring me in place, and my breath catches.

I don't pull away either. Can't.

Kai drops money onto the table, covering the cost of my untouched wine. The sound of it hitting the wood is sharp, final. Without another word, he threads our fingers together and leads me from the tavern.

The air outside is cooler than earlier today. In the horizon, the sun sets and the night blooms release a soft perfume, but it's dulled by the scent of man, wood, and that hint of sweetness from the pineapple that makes my mouth water. The combination is sexy, overpowering my senses in the most pleasant way, and I forget the world around us as he leads me silently down the street.

I'm not thinking about anything outside this stolen moment.

A mistake? More than likely, but I don't care. Not right now.

The further from the center of town we get, the more his body relaxes. The rigid control I felt radiating from him in the tavern loosens, shoulders lowering, and the line of his mouth is less severe. He doesn't release me, though. Instead, Kai moves my hand to the crook of his elbow, covering mine with his in a gesture that cannot be called anything but gentlemanly. *Sweet.*

I tilt my head up, caught by the sharp cut of his jaw. In the way his head turns just enough that our eyes meet again, and in them, the glint of hunger is unmistakable. It makes my heart beat faster and my pulse flutter, a rhythm I know he can hear.

"I've waited." Two words, and once again, they leave him in a dark, yet velvet tone. Man and wolf, their tone curling around me in a way that tugs at the center of me. Like a spell—a call—I can't ignore, and I find myself moving closer. In this moment, nothing matters but luxuriating in the heat coming off his skin and scent. His thumb brushes across my knuckles, testing the pulse flowing between us. "So fucking long. Even without the stone, I know."

Out of nowhere, two dogs run past us, almost barreling into me before I can make heads or tails of what he just said. I blink, and my back is against the wall of a closed bakery with Kai standing a few inches from me.

Not touching, but the heat coming off his large body envelops me like a blanket, and my nipples tighten against the soft cotton of my dress.

"Look at me, sweetheart."

"I'm..." I trail off, almost biting back a whimper when a soothing, low rumble comes from his chest. It's calming. Can't control my compliance—don't want to fight it.

I barely reach his chest, and to meet his gaze, I have no choice but to tip my face up. Those soulful eyes are staring at me, and I find myself fascinated by the change in them. One second brown, the next golden, and his gaze remains intense.

There's reverence in them, too.

My eyes lower a bit, and I notice the slightly crooked bridge of his nose, an imperfection that doesn't diminish his handsomeness. If anything, it adds to it. And as if he knows what I'm thinking, he lowers his head, bringing his mouth to my nose, and he kisses the tip.

Such a contrast to the rugged and dominant man I know he is. The filthy, untrustworthy pirate.

What are you doing, Nerissa?

Kai chuckles then, and the sound feels like a warm caress. It renders my earlier thought void, and I want him closer. To burn myself with his touch.

I'm in trouble.

"...I didn't reset it before my healing abilities kicked in."

"Oh," I say. Not the most eloquent reply, but I'd been too busy watching his mouth just now. How it moves with each enunciation. How he ran the tip of his tongue over his slightly fuller bottom lip.

Won't deny the small shiver that crests over me at the act. And while I should be embarrassed by my attraction to this man—an enemy to my people—I'm not.

Instead, I blush. Heat spreads across the apple of my cheeks, spreading down until reaching the tops of my breasts. Another mistake.

Alpha Kai watches me with undisguised hunger. His eyes roam, taking in each delicate bow where a button should be. From my bust to the hem of my mid-thigh summer dress, he doesn't miss a single detail. Raw and palpable need flows between us. The attraction is electric, and I find myself tightly sandwiched between his warm body and the wall on my next breath.

He's breathing hard, tattooed midsection heaving, and I've never felt so small in my life. So delicate.

Wetness coats my upper thighs, my core clenching hard when a strong arm slips around my waist and lifts me until we're face to face, chests drawing in deep breaths while his exhale becomes my inhale.

Gods help me. I cannot resist him.

Yet my prayer falls of deaf ears. More so when I get to experience a taste of his protectiveness.

A warning snarl suddenly rips from him, and the sound reverberates against my lips—they tingle in its wake. It also causes a few yips to come from somewhere around the corner; the response is one of fear and submission.

He's alert where I've been docile, ignoring the subtle tilt of his head, picking up conversations, and keeping track of where the residents are. Affording us privacy. It reminds me of my own abilities, how the lightest noise filters through, or how easily I should pick up movements. All normal behavior, especially from—

I'm stopped in my tracks.

From his intense eyes to his lips and then his neck, where I pause. *Where is it?* There's nothing where the stone should've been. Where just a few days ago, I'd seen the chain, a large black stone dangling and hard to miss.

That day, as he fought the rogue, I'd taken note of the size, the metal used to secure it, and began to plan. I was going to take it. Let nature distract him while I slip undetected onto his ship—a thunderstorm my cover—and then slip away back home.

Easy. Controllable. Magda was part of my plan; I needed her to create a scent blocker for me. My cloak would work; its ability to hide my scent and heat trace is unmatched, but there are too many variables that can go wrong.

It could snag on something.

It could be grabbed.

Two scenarios I'm unwilling to test. Not when this wolf is more than meets the eye.

Pricks of pain send a jolt of pleasure through me. It's his claws; they've extended, and when my gaze meets his again, his fangs are exposed. His grin is just shy of feral.

"I'm going on instinct, sweetheart. More beast than man, and I want you."

"Kai," I breathe out, a slip of the tongue as he hasn't given me his name. Haven't given him mine, either. Not that Alpha Daire calls me out on it. If anything, he revels in the way it rolls off my tongue. There's a vibration coming from his chest, that sweet little sound again, and it causes my core to clench and my hips to gyrate. *Fuck*, he's purring for me.

Throbbing against my mound, *but* then he lowers me, slowly rubbing himself over my midsection until my feet touch the ground. Thick, long—I'm whimpering as he removes his hand, tapping my nose with a single finger while a slick smirk graces his lip.

"Run, little treasure."

ALPHA KAI

NINE

That's all the warning I give her.

One step. Two steps. I take ten steps back, closing my eyes for a few seconds while I savor her need for me. She's everywhere. Her slick desire in the air between us and the sweet with a delicate-hint-of-salt perfection complements her naturally addictive perfume.

Floral. Fruity. *Mine.*

There's a subtle shift in front of me, the soles of her open-toed sandals dragging against the cobblestone beneath our feet. I'm attuned to the most minute movement, and when she moves closer instead of away, I snap my teeth at her playfully.

Her squeal—half shock, half laughter—slides across my every nerve ending like a pulse, and my eyes snap open. Moreover, the longer she's near, the harder it thrums through me, and I grunt in approval. The sound is full of pride, both man and beast, a low growl that causes goosebumps across her tanned skin.

That sinful blush also deepens from her cheeks to her bigger-than-a-handful breasts. They're encased in a soft, white cotton dress sans bra, and I can't help but let my eyes wander low. I follow the path of small bows down the front to where her cunt is hidden from view.

Are you bare for me, pretty girl?

Motherfuck, I'm hard. My cock thickens and pushes against the fabric of my pants. I can feel the beads of pre-come as they slip from the head and down the shaft before disappearing into the stitching. Anticipation and lust—a heady combination I welcome for the first time in my life.

Only for her. For the woman I will claim and mate.

"Run, little treasure."

"W-what are you—"

"Ten, nine, eight..." Before I get to seven, she bolts. Her dress flares around her thighs as she races down the street, heading in the direction of her house. Hair whipping. Hips swaying. The game of chase is exquisite, and I plan to indulge myself.

I've never touched a woman. Never felt the urge to break my vow to my goddess-given mate, but the way I react to her, I know she's mine. The same way she leans into me and softens at the sound of my purr is all the proof I need.

"We'll get the stone tomorrow," I say, stretching my neck side to side. "Tonight...we hunt."

My wolf's agreement comes in the form of a rippling awareness. Contentment.

I'll pick it up tomorrow before breakfast and explain.

I give her a small head start while my wolf stretches, savoring the trail of her scent and the unhidden arousal I plan to drown in. He agrees with me. It's there in the heightening of my senses and the coiling of my muscles, my weight shifting forward as we prepare to give chase.

Moreover, she gets as far as the end of the street before I give in to my impulses and half-shift. My clawed feet dig into the ground while I lick a fang, inhaling roughly before taking off after her.

And the moment I do, she looks back, nearly stumbling but rights herself as another delighted sound leaves the back of her throat. Not a scream. No fear. My female is excited.

And the faster she runs, pumping those lithe legs, the more I slow my gait. She's so much smaller than I am, and for every three of her steps, I take one, and she's never out of my view. Businesses give way to a winding road, and there's nothing on either side of us. Just grass, some patchy areas of sand, a small playground for those who have children here, two wooden ramps that lead to beaches—

Her home comes into view.

There's a small porch light on, its glow giving the front of her home some warmth, but she doesn't head inside. Instead, she bypasses the cottage and heads toward the back. More precisely, the jungle behind it. It's different than what you'd find in the southern or western sea, a denser forest, but the tropical vegetation here grows wild and heavy—palms, broad-leaf trees, and flowering vines that thrive in this damp heat.

It's darker now as she slips inside; the sun has fully set, and the varying shades of purple and orange have slowly become a dark blue. Almost black. A clear night, except for the sea of stars guiding her tiny steps past the thick tree line.

I stop at the edge a few seconds later.

While my wolf follows her every move, the way she dodges overgrown roots, I send a final mindlink to Torren on the ship.

Do not contact me unless it's an emergency. I'll be back at dawn.

Through the pack bond, I feel the weight of his unasked question, but Torren's trust outweighs his curiosity. If nothing else, he's loyal. Trustworthy.

Yes, Alpha. Enjoy your night.

Cutting the link, I lick my lips and catch traces of her desire. It's softer now; the breeze coming off the nearby water marks it with its salty brine, but I like the combination. The sea has always felt like home, even if I never spend time inside of it.

Wolves travel through, but never bathe in it. Sirens aren't to be trusted, and their king is a joke who hides beneath the water. The entire royal family does, including the future heir.

"You're slower than I imagined," she whispers, a coquettish lilt to her tone, and I laugh at the slight mock. We both know it wouldn't take much to subdue her, but I love the playfulness. Let her believe she has the advantage.

"What's your name, beautiful?" I call out, stalking her slowly like the predator I am while the jungle welcomes us. Humid and alive, its shadows curl around each tree. Every leaf, every rustle...it's the perfect backdrop as I follow her deeper into its cradle. She's a few minutes ahead of me, and yet easy to find.

Every gasp, every quick glance over her shoulder—her laughter that rings and reverberates—feeds my hunger. Branches scratch at her calves and leaves cling to her sweat-slick skin, but she doesn't care or stop. If anything, it's a challenge to push harder and see how long it'll take for me to catch her.

Those giggles will be my complete undoing.

This foreplay: a delicious game that taunts and teases until one of us snaps will have her marked before the sun rises.

Because there's no mistaking who will snap first.

We have the rest of our lives to get to know one another.

Tomorrow, when the sun rises and I wake her with my tongue, I'll ask questions and answer her, but for tonight, I plan to let the wolf have full rein. Because our animals aren't ruled by logic, but instinct, and every single one of mine is pulling me in her direction. Who and what she is doesn't matter.

I pick up my pace, muscles taut and senses alive. The distance between us closes, the tip of my black-tipped claw skims the back of her arm, and the squeal of delight she emits causes my knot to throb. For my cock to give a harsh jerk, and the head slips out of the half-closed zipper.

She sees this from over her shoulder, stumbling in the limited light, but rights herself at just the right moment before turning right.

There's a thicker crop of trees up ahead, almost maze-like, and she slips within the Ceibas and breadfruit trees. A couple of almond and guava trees are also present, but they flank the outer rim of this cropping.

"Name, sweet female?"

"You have to earn the right, Wolf." My beast likes the challenge. His chuffs mix with my laugh, and the sound reverberates through the jungle. More so when she finds refuge behind a large trunk, her front plastered to its bark. She's trying to be inconspicuous, but those violet eyes cannot be hidden.

They catch the moonlight, dim as it may be through the treetops, and I bite back a smile.

It'd be easy to snatch and mount her, take what is mine, but I don't.

Instead, I drag my claws across the closest tree trunk. The gouges I leave behind are jagged and deep, but it's the sharp splintering of wooden fibers that makes her run. From one Ceiba to another, even a palm if she ventures farther to the edge, while I watch.

Her heart rate speeds up, and her breathing is a bit labored, but it's the spike in her scent that has me fighting back a full shift. It's stronger now, spreading through each tree until reaching me, and the way it slides across my bare skin feels like the soft stroke of her hand. As if she were walking around me, dragging her finger over each muscle before dipping low.

From tip to knot, I pulse in time with her heartbeat. The *thump, thump, thump* is a cadence I walk toward while she moves again. I'm at the center of the cluster as she prances around me, hiding behind trees, while I let her think she's won.

"You're not good at this game, are you?"

"You're going to pay for that."

"I'm not afraid," she singsongs, making another change in position. A mistake. Her thought process, though cocky, trusted that this predator had become docile during our game. Thinking she could slip past me and escape my grasp. Another mistake.

One I will capitalize on. The second she rushes, I turn and pounce, slipping a hand around her waist as I lift her off the ground mid-sprint. What starts as a shriek quickly turns into giggles, but even those are cut off within seconds.

Her back meets the trunk of the nearest vine-covered tree, my body pinning hers in place.

I don't lower her, either.

We're not face-to-face, more like she's level with my upper chest, but she's high enough that with a quick dip of my face, I can kiss her. Not that she complains. Instead, this little treasure digs her fingers into my arm and arches up into me. There's just a thin bit of cotton separating her skin from mine, and yet her heat sears me.

Having her this close feels right.

"Whose bad at this game?" It leaves me in a groan when she manages to wrap one leg around my hip. The hem of her dress rises, more soft skin exposed, and I groan out as one hand traces from her knee to her upper thigh and back down again. "Tell me."

"I can admit defeat." She tries to hop and wrap her other leg around me and fails. Then she pouts, an unconscious act from the furrow of her brows and the way she looks down toward said leg.

Cutest fucking thing.

"Ask me."

"I don't—"

"Tell me what put that look on your face, and I'll fix it."

Understanding dawns, and once again she blushes. With my wolf's ability to see clearly at night, I catch the pink on the apple of her cheeks and the thin misting of sweat clinging to every inch of her. It's light, but hard to ignore when each drop that rolls down her skin is magnified decadence.

My fangs ache with the need to bite, but before I can at the very least nip her ear, she tips her face up and flutters her eyelashes at me. Slowly. Coquettishly. "Help me lift my leg."

Playfully, I snap my teeth a hair's breadth from her small button nose. "And place it where, little treasure?"

Those violet eyes narrow, and her lips purse. "You're enjoying this."

"I am. Not going to deny that."

"Please wrap my leg around your waist," she says, voice so sweet. Low and breathy.

A wish I grant, pressing my hard, half-covered cock against her bare pussy. The head grazes her slit, and we both pause, lust striking through me with the force of a battering ram.

I know there are things we need to discuss.

Who she is. What I am. Her fucking name...

But everything ceases to exist when she slants her mouth over mine and the tip of her tongue traces my bottom lip. The world could cease to exist, and I wouldn't give a single fuck.

All I hear and feel is her. Just her.

NERISSA

Ten

I shouldn't be doing this, but I can't walk away.

Not when he brings one hand to the back of my neck, gripping the strands while keeping me in place. His lips are on mine now, dominant and all-consuming, as if he needs me to breathe, and damn it all to hell, I need him too. Kai owns my first kiss, and my soul welcomes his claim.

It feels right. I'm right where I'm supposed to be, and it's more apparent than ever when the rumble in his chest moves through mine. "Fuck, sweetheart. This sweet little mouth will be my undoing."

Each vibration soothes while at the same time excites. I feel it from my lips down to my nipples before it settles on my clit, and I can't help but tighten my legs around his hips. The small gyration, each pleasure-seeking shift—

I'm rewarded by the feel of his large hand leaving my hip a second before the sound of fabric tearing follows. Then it's skin on skin. His cock, long and hard, is pressed against my core, and I clench hard.

A needy sound leaves me, desperate and demanding at the same time. "More. Please, more."

"Give me your name, little treasure."

"Why do you call me that?" It leaves me on a pant—the sound slipping from my mouth into his—and a throaty male groan is my reward. It sends shivers down my spine, more so when he slips his tongue inside and caresses mine again. He doesn't answer right away, but explores every inch with swipes and nibbles until I feel lightheaded, completely docile in his hold.

Then he pulls back just enough to meet my eyes, golden on violet. The wolf is staring back at me. "Because that's what you are. You're the kind of precious wonder men spend their lives searching for, and I don't share my treasures. I guard them, but more importantly, I'd kill anyone who ever coveted you."

"That's…" I swallow hard while my nipples tighten into tight, stiff peaks. The siren in me loves the possessive declaration. Needs it. "Thank you."

"Never thank me for being honest. Just honor me with your name."

"You did catch me."

"I did."

"But do you think you've earned the right?"

"Challenge accepted." A clawed hand lifts to the back of my head, gripping my dark hair in a tight fist while the tips simultaneously massage my skull with the most delicate pressure. I whimper, the sensation addictive, but accompanied by the feel of his hard cock pressed against my slick flesh, and I'm unable to resist.

His touch. The way he slams his mouth onto mine again, this time hard and fast and messy. Kai overpowers my rationality, not that there is much left, but the smidge I've been fighting to hold onto slips from my metaphorical fingers.

I'm wet, soaking my upper thighs and his engorged head, and the combined scent of our need is indescribable.

Everything about this moment feels right when I should be running.

Everything about this man will bring me pain, and yet I welcome the burn.

"Name?" Kai purrs, and the vibration makes my toes curl. For another rush of wetness to coat us, a reaction that he enjoys. It's there in the golden eyes staring at me as if I were a wondrous creature. In the way he snaps his hips forward, rubbing the swollen tip through my labia, bumping my clit on each pass. "Give it to me."

"Not yet."

"Name?" Not an alpha's bark, but the deep and dominating tone was more wolf than man. I can feel his powerful aura, its tethers sliding against my skin like a lover's stroke. My royal blood affords me this luxury; when others fear his bite, I welcome it.

Why do I crave it?

Yet before I can overthink it, I push that thought away and smile. "Make me."

My denial only excites him, and I'm turned around with my front facing the tree on my next breath. There's no time to react or complain; the sound of my dress tearing fills the night before a cool breeze sweeps past us. It lies in tatters near my feet while the moon appears brighter.

While I can still make out the sound of waves crashing upon the shore, and I know the water is shimmering a brighter blue.

My emotions have always been tied to the weather and sea; any shift signals a change, and in this moment, they're celebrating with me. I've never taken a lover, but not because it's against our laws— some choose to be wild and free before a mate ship happens, while others honor the bond.

I'm the latter.

I've always wanted to be pure for him or her, but this pull to Kai is undeniable. Even without the stone or its magic, my soul is calling out to his—demands I accept—and there is no stopping this. Him. Me. A pull that will destroy us; of that I have no doubt, and yet I don't care.

Selfish. Irresponsible. *I want him.*

Kai purrs against my nape, his lips trailing down my spine. He stops in between kisses to nip then lick, soothing the abused flesh on his exploration. Goosebumps rise and spread, my body thrumming with pleasure while the tree bark drags across my nipples with each minute shift.

It's torture. A tiny bite of pain with the pleasure.

My palms flatten against the rough bark; I'm trembling and full of anticipation, clenching my thighs to alleviate some of the ache he's created. I'm wet, naked, and at his mercy.

"Such a beautiful little treasure I've found. So pretty and pink and mine," he croons against my skin, his big hands gripping my hips and pulling me back toward him, bending me at the waist. From my new position, I see his knees on the ground right before one large hand spreads my knees further apart.

I tremble. I'm nervous and excited, and *oh God!*

The first swipe of his tongue makes my knees weak, forehead falling against the tree as a fully-body shiver runs through me. I've never experienced anything like this, not even when I've explored my body inside the privacy of my home here in Avaria.

There's a sense of freedom I have here.

Behind my closed door, no one can interrupt or walk into my room without a literal wall stopping them. Something our kingdom doesn't truly promote. Yes, we have *some* privacy, but not like this.

I'm addicted to the independence. To my rebellion from what's expected and not allowed.

His growl of satisfaction vibrates through me then; I feel it from my clenching hole to my clit, the latter of which throbs on his tongue. "Will you gift me your name now?" Each word is spoken against my sex, a little muffled while his exhalations warm my clit.

From the now cooler breeze to his hot breath, I enjoy the different sensations each one elicits. "Or do you need me to say *please*?"

That last word is accompanied by the flat of his tongue slowly sliding from my clenching hole to my bundle of nerves, and a low, mewling sound leaves me. I feel him shake—his grip on me tightens and those long claws break skin. Not too deep, but enough that a few beads of blood pool at the cut and then roll down my hip. There's a slight sting at the cut, but when he laps at my entrance, slipping the tip of his tongue inside and creating a delicious heat low in my belly, I find myself pushing back.

Fighting against his hold. Wanting more.

"Kai, that...oh my gods!"

"Good girl." Something about the praise tugs at the core of me. It's heady, and I almost preen, a reaction he can literally taste between my thighs. I can't help but look back at him from over my shoulder, even if the position is a little uncomfortable. And when I do, I see this glorious alpha on his knees—muscles bulging and fur bristling across his arms and chest—fighting back a shift...

I bare my siren teeth at him.

They're not as sharp as his, but I have predator instincts, and those golden eyes darken around the edges, honey at the center with a dark brown ring around the outer rim. I find them beautiful—a realization that unsettles me, a dangerous truth slipping past what little is left of my defenses.

But then he winks. A warning.

"Mine," Alpha Kai growls, fangs grazing my labia, pricking the flesh before deepening the kiss. And it's that bite of pain that shatters me, his hungry grunt as my blood and wetness bathes his tongue. He's a possessed man. Holding me up when my knees grow weak, he eats me through each shiver and clench, my walls pulsing in time with the flicks of his tongue. I come for him on a long and loud moan, my hand slamming against the tree as my hips ride his face.

I'm pushing back and trying to gyrate, riding the tidal waves of pleasure cresting through me. From the top of my head to my feet, I'm sensitive yet thrumming with the need of more.

I also don't realize that in the height of my orgasm, I'm whining my name. Over and over, giving him a prize for making me fall into a pleasurably painful bliss.

"Nerissa."

One word. Silken sin coming from the enemy's mouth tastes sweeter to me. In that moment, as another small rush of wetness coats my lips and drips down to the jungle's floor, I'm struck by another thought. *Does he know who I am?*

Would he still be on his knees for me if he did?

"Kai, I'm…of *fuck*!" I'm airborne for a moment, turned in his hands and laid on my back with his body covering mine, before the last syllable has passed through my lips.

"You know who I am." Not a question. The expression on his still-wet face—my come on his lips—is one of pride. His chest puffs out and rubs against my breasts, the thick yet soft hair there eliciting shivers from me that have nothing to do with the mild wind.

"I do, Alpha."

"What I'm capable of." Not a question but a statement. Acknowledging his ability to be kind and cruel.

"Yes."

"Motherfuck, you're perfect." His entire body shakes above me, the hand near my head slipping beneath to cup the back of my skull. His touch is soft and reverent as he rubs his thumb in a soothing circular motion over my pulse point. "I can scent your innocence, little treasure."

His teeth nip my neck while a single finger slips inside me to the second knuckle. When he retracted his claws, I don't know or care when the stretch feels so good. In and out in a slow motion—not deep, just testing—but then I feel the pressure. He pushes against my hymen, not hard but more of an acknowledgement.

"Don't stop." My hips buck up, trying to get him in deeper. "Please don't stop."

"I won't knot you today," Kai says, his expression serious. The words of an alpha. "Soon, though, you'll be locked with me while my mark is on your graceful neck. This is my vow to you."

"Pretty words," I say in a neutral tone, failing because there's no denying or hiding my excitement. How I clench around his finger or the warm rush of wetness that has nothing to do with my prior orgasm. *I like it too much. Want it.*

"An eternity chasing you will never be enough, Nerissa."

A needy, keening sound leaves me the second he pulls his finger out. "What are you—"

"Relax." Kai's hand makes a sharp movement. I feel the jerk of his arm, and then we're skin to skin. Nothing between us. His cock notches at my entrance, and my eyes roll back, whimpering when he dips it in and out before spreading my wetness from hole to clit and back again.

Seconds pass, and he continues to do so, never taking his eyes off me. He covers me with his heat while the damp grass beneath us creates the perfect contrast. But then he stops and lowers his face down to mine. Softly, he kisses me again, traces of me still on his lips. I like it, too.

Him and I.

Woodsy and floral, yet sweet. Yet behind every note, there's a touch of the sea. We both carry it, our scents melding perfectly together. *Meant to be.*

"Guide me in, little treasure." His words pull me from that thought, and for a second, I get lost in his hooded eyes. The heat in them, but there's also a sweet tenderness. "Take my cock and help me guide our first time."

"Are you...?" I trail off, but he nods.

"My wolf and I have never touched or claimed another female. No one but you." The salty ocean breeze filters through the trees, and I can hear the waves crashing not far from here, as it mixes with the damp earth and our combined scent. I've never felt daintier or more feminine, his body so large compared to mine, and it's further cemented when, with trembling hands, I wrap my fingers around his girth.

He's huge. Long and thick.

I place the engorged head against my soaked entrance, the tip just inside…

"Kai," I scream out when he buries himself to the hilt in one smooth stroke, pushing my hand aside. I'm hit with a tinge of discomfort, no true pain, and I thank my mermaid genetics for the gift of taking every inch without breaking. I feel stretched and will likely feel sore after, but there's a rightness to this moment. It's where I'm supposed to be.

Him. Me. We belong.

My body accepts him, tight fit as it is, and I'm rewarded by the throbbing of his cock against my tender walls. He's pulsing, each one feeling like a massage, and I'm surprised by the tenderness of his action.

Kai doesn't move. His body's tense above me, muscles coiled tight while a low *fuck* sweeps past his lips and onto my skin, skin he's peppered with kisses and nips, leaving tiny marks behind while his swollen knot rests against my labia. Not entering, but teasing my body with something I now crave.

There's no doubt in my mind; I was made to handle him. I want more.

"Please, Alpha." Another whine, and I'll examine the sound later. Much later, as it's not a sound mermaids make. "Stretch me. Ruin me."

"You naughty little thing." His claws are out again, and he traces his right hand from my hip to my breast. They leave a small, fiery trail in their wake, but when he flicks my pebbled tip—I clench hard. "I'm going to devote my life to your pleasure, Nerissa. My alter will be at the juncture of your thighs, and my home will be your pouty mouth."

"Kai, I…"

He shakes his head, taking my left nipple between his claws

and tugging on it. I feel it in my pussy, and so does he as I bathe him a moment later with my arousal. His reaction is automatic, pulling out slowly—I feel his veins throb—before thrusting back in.

Leisurely at first. No hurry, while my fingernails dig into his arms. That one stroke, and I'm trembling. Have no control over my lips as I undulate beneath his strong body.

Nothing has ever felt so good.

"Fuck, you're perfect." The hand cradling my head angles it, his mouth descending on mine. This kiss is possessive and hungry; he consumes me while his hips snap with force this time. So hard he moves me, my back sliding across the grass, and he follows, never pausing his strokes.

Now, he rides me fast and hard. It's a painful pleasure, sharp and intoxicating, holding me captive in a moment that I know will change everything.

I can't stop it. Don't want it to end.

All I can do is hold on tight, my thighs wrapping around his hips while my fingernails find purchase on his sides, breaking skin across his ribcage as he claims me. He's all I see and understand.

"So close. Gods, I'm close." His response is a hiss through clenched teeth; satisfaction resonates from him. It strums between his body and mine, and I'm in awe of it. As if there's an invisible string connecting us.

I'm a part of him, as he is a part of me.

A revelation that shocks me, and I cry out, trying to speak, but nothing intelligible comes out. I'm reduced to moans and whimpers —the needy sound of a female lost in nirvana. Nothing could feel better than this...

But then I'm flipped onto my hands and knees, his large frame covering mine. I have no strength to raise my hips. I'm a mess of shaky limbs, and Kai chuckles at the sight.

Knees part mine to accommodate him, my legs forced up until I'm exposed and my wetness is dripping onto the grass below. There are leaves in my hair, specks of dirt on my skin, and yet I've never felt more beautiful.

"Fuck, sweetheart. Your blood looks good on my cock," he groans, and the sound of skin on skin, a slow *fapping* sound, greets my ears. My head snaps to the side, and I meet his honeyed eyes over my shoulder. Stroking himself, his heated gaze roams from my face to where I need him most. "It's a privilege to be your first, and you mine. No woman before you, and there will be no one after, Nerissa. I'm yours."

"Mine." Possessive. That's what I feel toward him at the moment, as if I'd kill anyone who touched him. *He's the enemy—*

With our stares locked, he strokes twice, a movement I follow before notching himself at my entrance. Then he slams back in, his hold tight, and I know there'll be some bruising.

Moreover, I'm grateful that my mermaid abilities will heal me quickly, but for a few hours, I'll revel in each dark circle where his fingers or claws dug in.

His pace is hard and brutal, fucking me into the ground with deep pumps, each deep stroke driving his thick head against that tender spot, one that causes electrical pulses to fire across my processors. It's heaven and hell; I'm chasing the feeling and want it harder, a silent demand he answers.

I try to brace my arms but fail, once, twice, before his body fully covers mine until there isn't an inch of me not blanketed. "Yes. Oh Gods, yes."

"Not a god, little treasure. I'm your alpha." Another brutal punch of his hips, and his unoccupied hand grips my hair. He gathers the long strands in his fist, tightening his hold before turning my face. "That's it, Nerissa. Tighten around my cock...let me feel you break for me."

The moon is high and the trees filter its light, leaving behind a soft shimmer that cloaks us in secrecy. Out here, it's just us, and I'm at peace under him.

These sensations are new and overwhelming, a little painful, yet it's the feel of his teeth at the back of my neck that causes me to freeze. My muscles clench tight. My breath catches in my throat. And when he breaks the surface of my skin, not a full bite, but a tear, I come for him.

For a second, I'm blinded by the waves of bliss coursing through me. They're not gentle or soft, each burying me in a sea of heightened bliss and an awakening I can't undo.

"That's it. Take my cock like a good girl, Nerissa." Kai's gritted demands are accompanied by three sharp punches of his hips, forcing me to take every solid inch, but not his knot. That sits outside my opening, throbbing against my sensitive skin, tearing a scream from my throat. The feel of him there, how the bulge pulses, sends the ripple of another orgasm through me, and this time, Kai follows.

I'm filled and dripping, each spurt longer than the last, and he's not done.

Exhaustion settles in while he continues to slip in and out slowly, draining every last drop until finally settling in and turning us to our sides so I'm not crushed. His length jerks a few times, now and then there's a smaller dribble of come, and I close my eyes, savoring the moment.

Tomorrow will come with plenty of problems, but for now, I give in and let the feel of his warm body lull me into sleep.

The last words I hear before succumbing tug a small smile from me...

"Let's get you cleaned up and tucked in, little treasure. Because in one hour, I'll make you my dirty girl all over again."

ALPHA KAI

ELEVEN

A　*lpha, we're under attack!*

　　I'm pulled from my sleep by the sudden shout in my head. For a moment, I'm disoriented, inside a room I'm not familiar with, but then her scent hits me. Orange blossoms, coconut—me. My scent is all over the wondrous creature beside me, her face peaceful in her slumber.

Then again, she hasn't had much time to rest.

I gave her the promised hour, then fucked her for two hours straight. Another short break, and I had her cock-drunk body in the shower, claiming her again while the steam clung to our skin. On her back in the living room, sprawled beneath the wall-to-wall shelves overflowing with books and an odd collection of trinkets.

On all fours in the hallway, when I couldn't control myself, the sway of her enticing hips too much of a temptation. And finally, just two hours ago, I had her draped over me in this bed, riding her slow, spanking her ass, and guiding her exhausted body to meet me thrust for thrust.

Alpha, the merman general just…

Torren's communication is cut off, and I'm on my feet, waking Nerissa in the process. I'm not worried about my nakedness, but I still grab a pair of pants I'd picked up after I put her to bed after the last round. The shifter's clothes box was close enough that I couldn't have been gone longer than three minutes.

I'm on my way. Kill anyone who boards the ship.

"Where are you going?" she asks, sleepily rubbing her eyes. Rumpled and with a few lines from the pillow on her cheek, Nerissa truly looks adorable. Walking over, I bend low enough to reach her lips and place a peck on them. Suck on the lower one just a little bit before pulling back. "One more, Alpha."

I do, but this time lay a tiny kiss on her forehead, my hand caressing her cheek. "I'll be back. Get some more sleep."

"But—"

"Trust me, I'll be back."

"What's wrong?" Nerissa's brows pucker, her hand grabbing mine. "Did something happen?"

Surrounded. Two hurt.

"I'll be back." Ignoring the concern on her face and the call of my name, I leave her room and I'm out the door within seconds, my wolf bursting through and landing on his paws just outside her property line. He's angry, and so am I, but we still turn and look at her door when we sense her standing there.

Something is wrong with her expression; there's worry and a touch of sadness—guilt. The latter of which makes no sense, especially since she's done nothing wrong.

I'll be back and will soothe her.

I will not leave her. She's mine, my mate and future, and nothing will take her from me. The stone is irrelevant; my wolf and I already know the truth. It's carved into our bones. She belongs at my side, and I'll make sure that's a reality no matter the cost.

When the time comes, I'll place the Cordis Lux in her hands, not as proof, but as my vow—it'll be hers until the day our heir claims his birthright.

My wolf agrees. Happy, yet it's tempered with our gamma's earlier mindlink.

Disrespect isn't something I tolerate. To trespass upon my ship is unforgivable, but to attack it? That's a death sentence, one I'm the judge, jury, and executioner of.

Gamma, open the link. Let me hear.

Immediately, there's shouting. The sound of heavy footfalls and rapid movement—the clink of metal striking metal.

Where the fuck is it? The voice that comes through isn't Torren's. It's slightly higher in pitch and entitled, yet beneath the false bravado, I can detect fear. The slight tremor at the end gives him away.

I'm going to gut you and display your filthy remains at the bow of our ship.

I tear across town and to the port, every muscle coiled tight and paws hammering the cobblestone street and then the planks of Port Avaria's dock. My pants, which had been clenched between my teeth, are now somewhere behind me as I reach the edge.

Instincts are a dangerous thing, and when you hurt a predator's family, they're merciless. Unforgiving.

I jumped onto the ramp and into my ship, teeth bared and claws scraping wood.

The air reeks of salt and blood, and my senses flare—pain, fear, and the scent of my pack mingled with those of mermaid bodies. One siren is dead, an older man with a decorated kelp sash across his chest. His blood spreads across the old wood, tainting everything with his life's essence, which to me is worth less than that of a dead rat.

Then my eyes find Torren's. He's bleeding, the jagged edge of an armored glass protruding from his flank. He's hurt, bleeding, still standing his ground, and I jump in front of him without hesitation.

A growl rips through my chest, full of ire and promised

retribution, while mermaids swarm the ship. Their army chants, less a siren's song and more of a clicking sound—a war cry as they use their sharp nails to climb my vessel.

Their skins holds a faint glimmer under the sunlight, tails thrashing, creating a thumping sound as they push their way up. It's loud. Irritates my wolf, and he grabs the arm of the one closest to us and bites down, shattering his arm before tossing him aside.

He lands with a sickening crunch against the railing before slipping through and disappearing beneath the small waves.

And to my great pleasure, it silences the annoying *thwack*. What tries to climb aboard now is human skin: legs, arms, and not a single scale can be seen. Not even the shadow of one.

"Not one more filthy fucking merman on this ship. Understood?" Their alpha's command is met with a low, *Yes, sir.*

Those who try to leap past my men are beaten back by iron bars or wooden planks. The salty port air is filled with cries, howls, and the satisfying crack of bones as their army is met with force.

Ire. Hostility.

My attention turns back to the men standing a few feet from me: a nobody guard and then their general.

Orion is a figure of over-bloated elegance and a rotten core. We've met before, the few from the siren kingdom that show their pompous faces, and the narcissistic self-importance comes from his flesh in waves.

It's a pungent stench. Like an old, sick fish, and I catalog that fact for later.

He smells as though he's rotting from within.

"Stupid move, General."

"I see it as brilliant," he counters, hand gripping his sword tight. And in that grip, a flash of metal catches my eye.

My chain.

"Your blood will stain my claws, Orion," I growl, low and vicious. "Your ripped throat will lie at my feet before the sun has reached its highest peak."

Gamma Torren steps up beside me. In his hand, there's a fisherman's spear, and its deadly point is already bloody. "He was caught by Ewan and Oren sneaking out of your private quarters. They were ambushed from behind, but their growls alerted the crew who'd been eating below deck. I was checking supplies."

The two he mentions are injured. Breathing, but knocked unconscious near the gunwale while the rest of my pack fights like the proud beasts they are. Some have shifted, jaws snapping and grabbing the intruders in their maw and ripping chunks out before tossing them overboard.

Every strike from my wolves sends a thrash of mermaids tumbling back into the water, but more keep climbing. Their claws dig into the wood, hissing with rage.

I don't pause.

I lunge at Orion, shifting my attack at the very last second, going for his shoulder instead of his hand. It would be too predictable, and I want his hand holding the sword to be rendered useless. His scream rends the air a seconds before his blood drips from my fur.

The chunk I ripped falls from my mouth and lands with a splat, pulling a wolfish grin from me.

"You'll never keep her, mutt," Orion hisses from between clenched teeth, blue eyes glowing brighter. His head also tilts, as if hearing something in the distance, and his grimace quickly turns into amusement. An expression of sick satisfaction creeps onto his face.

Before I can ask what he means, I hear my gamma grunt in pain, his feet staggering back, and there's a new cut, this time on his chest. A straight line from one pectoral to the other, but it's not deep.

It'll burn, but there won't be a scar after he heals. Not even a faint trace within an hour.

It does serve to piss him off, though, and he grabs the soldier holding the small blade by the neck, slamming him headfirst into the wall nearby. Blood streaks down the old wood, the semi-conscious merman slumping until my gamma holds his entire weight off the ground.

A weight he disposes of with a quick toss to his left. He goes overboard, his limp form taking two other mermen with him.

Yet for every fallen, three more appear, and my men are bloodthirsty and ruthless. Teeth and claws—those in human form swing their weapons, striking anything that isn't pack and family.

Orion's sword flashes in my periphery, its sharp blade missing my shoulder. It grazes, but no damage is done, and I lunge, raking my claws across his face.

Then his neck, but he's smart enough to move back before I slice deep enough to hit any arteries. Dark blood oozes, his frantic eyes swinging right to left while I stalk forward.

My lips are curled back, and my blood-tipped claws are dragging across the deck.

"She's mine, Daire. She'll never accept you." The who he's talking about, I give no fucks about. At the moment, all my beast and I understand is eliminating this threat.

Taking back what's mine.

An answering snarl rips from my throat, lips curled back over my blood-stained teeth. I advance, and for every step I take, he retreats. There's a nervous energy all around him. I can taste his fear in the air, but then it all stills.

His army withdraws; one by one, they're falling back and over the railing, shifting into their tails and putting distance between them and my ship. Orion leaves, too, but not before tossing the stone overboard. His retreat is less cautious and more of a desperate dive—I try to catch him mid-jump—but I'm stopped in my tracks by the sight in front of me...

Nerissa is in the water, her eyes on mine, and in them I see the truth. She's also holding my necklace, and the stone dangling from her delicate fingers flares—black surface igniting into a fiery blue, as though flames lick and dance beneath the surface. The light is bright, wild, and uncontained, matching the ire in my chest.

Mates.

I am hers. She is mine.

And yet the betrayal burns just as bitter on my tongue, and my hands grip the railing, splintering the wood. When did I shift? I don't know or care; my instincts are zoned in to kill.

I watch as Orion swims up and tugs on her arm, moving her further away, and the once-bright Cordis Lux dies at his touch. I watch as those violet eyes dim. She nods, but then mouths, *We can't.*

My response? I wink.

That's it. Nerissa is in my blood now, our bond semi-formed, and I'll find her and the stone.

Both belong to me.

She's mine to worship and discipline; this betrayal won't go unchecked. That stone is more than its magic. It was the gift from a woman who broke the heart of an honest wolf.

I'll see you soon, little treasure.

NERISSA

Twelve

The water in Marivelle is cool against my skin, the unsettled currents brushing against my scales as I lie in bed. It's been twenty-four hours since his honeyed eyes glared at me, his mistrust thick in the air, and even from the water below, it struck with the force of a lash. Kai thinks I helped Orion, and while untrue, the stone *is* around my neck.

Something I'd been planning anyway, so why does it leave such a bitter taste on my tongue?

I'm angry. Hurt. Confused. Unable to think of anything but him as sunlight fractures through the surface for the first time in hours, the broken gold rays dancing across my tail.

My emotions have been as tumultuous as the storm above, the water violent, and I can't stop touching his chain—wishing its weight would anchor me. Instead, the Cordis Lux feels heavy, and its surface is cold. Like a heavy noose, and bringing it home did nothing to calm the storm within.

I'm in no hurry to hand it over. I'm irate at the mere thought of anyone touching what he wore close to his heart for so long.

He's a werewolf.

My mate. The one soul meant to be mine, and he has to be the enemy.

I can't accept him.

No matter how much every fiber of my being demands I return, slip beneath his warm body, and surrender to his bite. Mark *him,* my fangs leaving the sacred imprint of our bond for the world to see.

Because I want Alpha Kai Daire. There's no denying it.

Mates are sacred, and the Gods never make a mistake. Our souls are intertwined in a way that no man or beast can undo, and yet, I have no choice but to turn my back against destiny.

Our paths were set ablaze by his grandfather's greed and my grandmother's soft heart.

"He's a part of me," I whisper into the empty room, my lips moving, but barely a sound escapes. Because if heartbreak had a name, this moment is the very definition.

Guaiac wood. Leather. Pineapple.

That's what my mate smells like, and the memory alone is addictive. The perfect balance of tropical with a woodsy spice; it lit my soul on fire after the first inhale. My scales vibrated beneath his touch then, and they vibrate now as I recall the scent sliding across my senses.

I will never forget that first inhale. That wolf is forever etched into me, woven into my DNA.

Closing my eyes, I let the currents cradle me. Bubbles rise lazily past my hair, the silk of it floating around my shoulders and ribs while my heart races, each beat echoing within the stone against my chest.

Even here, beneath the waves, I feel him.

His presence on my skin lingers like the shadow of a storm, fierce and consuming.

Happiness at finding my mate. Sadness at being tied to an enemy of my people. And at the end, I'm right where I started...

Ire. Sorrow. Betrayal.

"Let's get this over with," I sigh, slipping from the bed, not bothering to glance at the mirror propped up in the corner. A tidehopper's trinket my grandfather tolerates at best. Our prior king, his father-in-law, despised anything from the surface, banning their use after salvagers first dragged the reflective glass through the palace's gates. They'd been searching for gold and steel—anything of worth—and instead, found their faces staring back.

Great-grandfather called them dangerous; vanity made distractions.

But when his only daughter accepted his general as her husband, Atlas bent the rules to keep her happy. She'd been curious, admired the way light reflected off the shiny surface—the truth they showed.

And as a wedding gift, my grandfather presented her with one. Gilded oval and with a delicate filigree, the piece is beautiful and kept inside her private sitting room.

Now, it's a common occurrence to see one. That, and brushes. Pretty baubles to fill pretty corners...

Swimming out of the room, I make sure to keep my eyes straight ahead and not give in to temptation. My reflection will only betray me, the red in my eyes nothing more than a mirrored image of the storm inside my chest. Truths I'm not ready to face.

It's better to be unguarded than broken.

I reach the royal dais at the heart of the palace, finding my grandmother seated on her throne. The water shimmers, bending around her as she smiles down at me, a frail silhouette of the woman I've always admired.

Her violet eyes, so much like mine, just a few shades darker, have a sheen of glass over them. The tears don't fall when we're underwater, only while on land, and yet they gather just the same. "Nerissa, why have you returned?"

I'm surprised by the question, and my back straightens in a defensive stance. "Because this is my home."

"Is it?" Her voice carries strength, yet layered beneath is a tremble that ripples across the distance separating us. "Or did you take what isn't yours, and now you hide from the repercussions?"

"This belongs here. To you."

"Or maybe it was meant to lead you down a different path." Her exhale is heavy, and for a few seconds, I feel shame. A loss that isn't mine, yet buried deep in my bones, I experience it just the same. "That heaviness is what I carry every single day. The loss is real."

"I don't understand. I-I thought you…" My words trail off, yet I still lift the stone around my neck out toward her. It vibrates against my skin. "This is yours—"

"To give, Nerissa." Grandma Lucienne lifts a delicate hand to stop me from removing the piece, but I do so anyway, swimming closer. I stop next to her chair and lean down, placing my forehead against hers, giving her my love and respect while placing the Cordis Lux in her palm. Mine encloses both, and immediately her bottom lip trembles. "Old friend, so honest and pure."

"Reclaim your magic and heal yourself, my queen. Please, I can't lose you."

She's the closest thing I have to a mother. Always there to guide and love, give reproach from time to time, but a constant in my life. Whatever's draining her, taking the vivacious, happy mermaid who raised me, has turned her into a frail woman. Her scales have dimmed, her face is now pallid, and no sea witch has been able to diagnose her.

No herb has stopped the sickness from spreading, either.

"This was never meant to be yours, Neri. I sent you to the surface for a reason, not to reclaim my gift to Ephraim."

"A gift? He stole from you!"

"Or maybe his fated mate gave him the only thing she could, so that no other wolf in his bloodline would experience the same devastation. The pain of losing the other half of their soul."

Her truth runs into me with the force of a killer whale slamming into you. It happened once when I was fourteen summers, playing with friends, and I swam out toward an injured, blue whale calf. It took weeks: a couple of healing potions and the resetting of bone for me to bounce back.

And yet, this feels worse. So much worse.

"What does that…what are you—"

"The Gods have not forgiven us, child." Her lips tremble, her expression one of pure grief, and the currents around us shift. Push a little more violently, as if renewed, yet uncertain. "It breaks my heart to see this again. To feel it pulse against our palms, but this magic… it's not ours to command, even if its origins come from me. The stone remembers its keeper, and what you hold now is unstable. Incomplete, and needs to go back to the wolves who care for it.

I swallow hard. My scales vibrate with a low hum, their shimmer faltering. "How can I help? Tell me, and I'll make it happen."

The water around us seems muted in my despair. It feels my sadness. I'm beginning to see that I'm more than lost, that I've been lied to, and information has been withheld.

She claims our family heirloom was a gift, while my grandfather wants to save his wife. *Somebody is lying.*

"What I am is wasting away, my child. This is the penance for a love deferred; the cost of the choices I made to protect my people and save *him.*"

"Him?" I ask, but I already know the answer.

"Ephraim Daire."

She was mated to a wolf.

I'm mated to a wolf.

Same bloodline. Same story.

History repeats itself.

"Enough," a voice booms from outside the hall, seconds before he steps in. Regal. Commanding. King Atlas glides forward with deliberate motion, eyes shifting to his wife before locking on me with calculated scrutiny.

Behind him, Orion and Naia of all people follow, and I'm more than confused. *What is she doing here? With them?* Their expressions are blank, yet tension radiates from her in pulsing waves.

I've known her since we were babies, growing up and getting into trouble together, trained by my father to fight and protect—the same way our army does. And yet, seeing her standing next to my grandfather feels like a betrayal.

The air vibrates with expectation, and I stay quiet. If they came to find me, they'll make the first move.

Not that he waits long. King Atlas swims toward his wife, dropping a kiss on her forehead. "That name is forbidden, my love. You know this."

"To some," our queen answers calmly, fin sawing back and forth. On the outside, she seems calm, but I notice the twitch of her fingers beneath mine. The flash of anger in her eyes just before she pushes the Cordis Lux back into my hand and nods for me to step back. Her movements are subtle, as is the urgent look she gives me. "You know this."

"To all, my queen. I'm a jealous merman." He sits beside her, ignoring her response and what I now know is a jab, and takes her hand in his. Only then does he turn his attention fully on me. "You've done well, my child. Thank you for returning the stone to its rightful owner."

"Did I?" There's a challenge in my tone; I'm not ready to deal with him. "Because I feel—"

"You and Orion did an excellent job, Granddaughter. I'm so proud of you." While his tone appears proud, the undertone of warning is there. It says to leave it alone. "We will honor you both under tomorrow's moon. The ballroom is being prepared as we speak."

I ignore the proclamation and raise a brow. "Why was Orion in Port Avaria? Under whose orders?"

"Mine," he says. Calm. Unbothered.

"*Why* was he following me?" My acerbic tone bothers Orion, and he stomps his polearm with the twin forked blade. Its heavy and strong staff is made of basalt stone, and the sound reverberates throughout the room. Icy and daring me to continue, much like his glare. "Is there a problem, General?"

"Respect the crown, Nerissa." Not yelled or hissed at me, but I still bristle at the reproach. So does my grandmother, but before she can say anything, I do.

I glide toward him and stop inches from his face. My eyes meet his, and it's hard, but I bite back a smile when I take note of his injury. He should've never messed with my wolf. *Control yourself, Nerissa. Kai isn't yours.*

"Or what?" Two words, simple and honest, and spoken just as coolly as he did to me a few seconds ago. "I am not beneath you, General Orion." The use of his name and title is on purpose. For someone who thinks highly of himself and is a firm believer in hierarchy, I just punched him where it hurts. "I will never justify my actions to you, much less my personal relationship with my family. Those do not, and never will, concern you."

That bothers him. His jaw clenches, eyes flicking to my grandfather for a minute before softening when meeting mine again. "My apologies, Princess. I'm just—"

We're interrupted by a sudden knock at the door. It's sharp and insistent; my scales ripple with unease. I hear my grandfather call for the person to enter, feel my grandmother's tired body slide in beside mine, and then feel all eyes on me.

Yet none of it matters as a guard delivers the news that my father's been found unresponsive beside my mother's memorial, his slumped body clutching a single pearl in his grip.

And if I thought my heart hurt before, I'm in agony now.

"Please..." my voice breaks, a sob catching in my throat "...take me to him."

Alpha Kai

THIRTEEN

The wolf in me howls as she fades beneath the water, while the man stands still, bottle of rum in my hand. Not drinking, just grabbed it from a nearby barrel before reaching the gunwale to watch the water calm after her disappearance.

An hour has passed now.

I'm angry and thinking—fighting against the urge to call out her name. It sits on my tongue, my instincts daring me to deny her, but the bitterness is hard to swallow.

Nerissa.

A blessing and a curse on my tongue, a taste I can't wash away no matter how much I wish it so. No amount of rum will help. No amount of blood staining these old, wooden floors will satisfy the betrayal I feel.

My fists clench at my sides, nails biting into my palms until I feel the sting of skin breaking.

I should have known. The signs were there...

Her decadent scent carried a hint of salt at the edge of each note.

In the hours I spent between her thighs, a light mist of water clung to her skin. I mistook it for sweat, the workout of a rough ride, but it tastes different now.

Like a dewy morning at sea: everything you touch or drink bears the brine of the ocean, a taste I've always craved—enjoyed from a young age as a weakness—yet now the connotation sits differently.

The fates have truly fucked me.

She's a siren.

Delicate. Beautiful. Dangerous.

Motherfucking perfection.

Every inch of this sultry nymph with the coquettish smile calls to me. She's designed to make men fall to their knees and worship, and yet the Gods have given her to me—a gift and a curse I accept without pause or doubt.

She belongs to me as I do her, even if, at the moment, I abhor who she is.

My weakness. My home.

Mate, a four-letter word that knocks my world off its axis. I no longer belong to myself, but give freely to a woman who's already betrayed me.

The wolf howls, the angry sound ripping from my chest, and the crew around me bare their necks. They don't understand just how deep this cuts, how my wolf demands I dive in after her and bring her back. Kicking and screaming don't matter, and if I kill every scaled bastard who helped her steal from me, even better.

True justice isn't sweet, but drenched in blood.

My body tenses, ready to leap—consequences be damned—but I fight back the reaction. The man understands what the wolf fails to: below the sea's surface is not my battleground. *Not yet.*

"Captain?" Otto's voice cuts in. He's the youngest crew member on board and Torren's brother. He's wary of me right now, standing back as if he's unsure of my reaction.

"Speak."

"How do you want—"

I tear my gaze from the dark waters, my jaw aching from the grinding of my teeth. "We leave port now. Ready the ship."

"Yes, Alpha." The crew surges into motion, while he makes his way to his brother—my friend. Lanterns swing, ropes groan, and sails unfurl while boots thunder against the deck. Voices remain low all around me, but each station master calls out to the other as the ship's prepared to undock.

"I'm fine," Torren tells his brother, his body braced against the mast. His shirt is torn and bloody through, yet the wounds are already clotting. Still raw, but healing, and my fury reignites at the sight.

"Let me help you." Otto tries to slip a hand around him, trying to take on his weight to move Torren, but the latter waves him away. The idiot reopened the stab wound; it bleeds sluggishly down his side, and his face pinches tight.

"Stop—"

"Gamma," I call out, and whatever bullshit he'd been about to spew dies on his tongue. I'm in front of him in an instant, cataloging his pale skin and the sweat dripping down his temple. Torren tries to push upright, stubborn ass, but the effort makes him stagger.

"Alpha, I'm fine," he grits out, fingers stained crimson where he touched his side.

"You're a piss-poor liar." That earns me a snort that ends in another grimace. For a second, my gaze flicks to the other two pack members lying on the deck, the onboard doctor checking injuries.

One seems to be out cold, with a swollen knot near his temple, while the other has a gash on his cheek. It's begun knitting together, the skin layers tightening, but the process is slow.

Both will be fine.

"Get them below," I bark, and another crew member shifts from his duties of tying down supplies to helping pick one of the injured up, carefully throwing him over his shoulder.

"Should've killed the bastard before he pulled out his blade,"

Torren groans low, and my head snaps to his. His expression is one of self-reproach. "I'm sorry, Alpha. I failed you."

No. That's my cross to bear.

"That kill belongs to me, Gamma, but I'll give you a consolation prize once you're back on your feet." Torren looks like he wants to argue, but a low growl from me stills him. "You are of no use to anyone bleeding out. Do not be stubborn, my friend."

His wolf rises, beast in his eyes, and they both nod, conceding the point. They also bare their neck in a show of respect.

"Otto, get him below deck and attend to him."

"Yes, Alpha."

As they make their way, careful not to further injure Torren, the ship moves away from the dock and into open waters. For a second, I close my eyes and enjoy the breeze and satisfying mist coming off the water until my wolf pushes against my skin again.

He wants control. To break free when behind closed lids, I see those gorgeous violet eyes. Remember running my fingers through her inky, black hair with the softest waves in each strand. How she came apart from my touch and cried out for more after each round.

In my thirty-three years walking this earth, nothing could've prepared me for her.

For the lightning bolt of need and hunger, the acceptance that this slip of a girl now belongs to me. Man and beast want her. Throb for her. *Nothing can change that.*

I can still taste her on my tongue; this unique blend of salt and sweet that's currently licking at my flesh as if her essence were a whip, marking me. Owning me.

I hate her for what she's done. Because—had she been honest—I would've given her the Cordis Lux and so much more.

I want her more than air, and it's a truth that burns me until I'm choking on this sin.

She's mine. There's no changing that, and Goddess help me, I will never forsake her.

The town's harbor fades behind us, and I grip the bottle still in my hand until my knuckles turn white. Until the glass cracks and shatters at my feet. A thousand tiny shards surround me, some producing cuts, but I couldn't give a fuck as I watch the horizon for any sign of her.

Nothing. She's gone.

And me? I'm left with no other option but to stand and then pace, repeating the action while rage cuts one way, and need the other.

It's in those moments as the ship breaks through the waves and daylight turns to night that I make a vow to myself.

By fang and sea, I will find her and rip the truth from her sweet lips before reclaiming what's rightfully mine...

But first, I need answers.

Days blur as the sea carries us home. While the crew tends to the wounded and daily shores, I steer and then pace. Then steer some more until it's time to rest.

I'm a ticking time bomb. Set to go off, and haunted by my dreams.

She welcomes me into her arms every night when I close my eyes, her sweet tone carrying through the tides, while I awake with her name on my lips. I'm hard and throbbing, sweat slicking my skin, and the ache grows heavier with each day that passes.

A physical manifestation of missing one's mate.

When Isle de Lobos rises from the horizon a few days later, my heart clenches tight for a different reason. This is home. My people, who I've let down.

The cliffs rear up jagged from the sea, and black stone was carved by years of storms. A large jungle spills from the island's heart—full of trees and wildlife—while smoke curls from the pack's hearth fires as they await our return.

My domain. My family.

On the shoreline, I make out my beta waiting. He's been made aware of our return by the watchers, wolves who welcome and report on activity beyond our shores.

Veris smiles as we near, broad and steady, a wolf carved of iron and one I trust with my life. He should've been with me on this run, but his mate was too close to her due date, and his place was here, welcoming his pup—a new life—into the pack.

"Alpha." He shows me his neck as I step onto the dock, the exhausted smile of a new father on his face. "My little Ophelia is strong and healthy with the cries of a warrior. Martha rests well."

I clap his shoulder, pride mixing with relief. "Congratulations, cousin. May she be blessed by the goddess, and her howl one day shake the mountains."

"Thank you, Kai. That means a lot to us." The smile drops from his face when he sees the three injured disembark, still a little weak. The glass pulled from Torren's side needs to be examined for poison. "What the hell happened? You just went to pick up supplies and your sword—"

"Send word to my father and grandfather. I want them in the stone hall immediately."

His brows furrow, catching the bite in my tone, but he doesn't ask. My beta nods, then rushes off to help his brethren and tell the prior alphas that they've been summoned.

The stone hall sits at the heart of the island, carved from volcanic rock long before my time. It's where all alphas, past and present, meet with their elders or pack members with leadership roles. Even visiting territory chiefs meet here when I summon them to discuss treaties or intercept bad judgment calls—the removal of someone who oversteps.

This is for diplomacy, while Isle San Tico is where I spill blood.

When I step inside its sacred walls, the torches dance. Shadows move, and the silence is as still as my father's position near the wall. His arms are crossed, face serious, while my grandfather sits like a king without a throne. Old, but unbroken, and his eyes are as sharp as the day he taught me about wolves and magic.

I don't waste time.

"Did you know?" I ask them, my tone hard. A tinge of bitterness coats each word. "Did you know my mate would be a siren?" Neither speaks, but my father shifts uncomfortably. Minute as it is, I catch the twitch of his hands and the small shuffle back of his feet. My grandfather, though, the old wolf, doesn't react. Instead, his gaze on me is steady and unblinking. "Why?"

"Son, you need to understand that—"

"They have the Cordis Lux. The stone is gone."

At that, a look passes between both men, and for the first time in years, my grandfather looks unsettled...

ALPHA KAI

FOURTEEN

E phraim Daire is a strong wolf.

He's noble and just, a little demanding, but I've never seen him like this. A pained expression crosses his face before his eyes darken and the fine hairs on his arms become a thick pelt as his wolf pushes forward. Not out of protective instinct, but because something pains him on a deeper level.

It pours from him.

Pain. Regret. Rejection.

And while I'm not an empath, as the alpha, I'm attuned to every member of my kingdom's emotions if I concentrate on a single individual. This is something that comes in handy to help soothe a wolf in distress or who is going through the loss of a loved one—the latter is what I sense in him.

A loss he's never gotten over.

"Answer me, Grandfather." I'm trying hard to rein in my anger and disappointment; my beast is on edge. Between his emotions and mine—and my father's worry—my tight leash is beginning to slacken, and claws, fangs, and fur burst forth. My muscles bulge, and in my half-shift form, I'm towering over everyone inside this room before my next low snarl. "Did you know our union was a possibility?"

"Yes." Ephraim's jaw tightens, but his eyes remain steady on me with a darkness I've never seen before. His eye contact isn't in defiance or disrespect, but to show honesty. The torches sputter as a breeze sweeps in from the open windows, casting a jittery light across his tired face. *His burden is heavy.* "It was always a possibility, one I worried about. First with your father, and then with you."

"What were you thinking, keeping something like this from me?"

"That my prayers were answered, and the goddess held no ill will toward me or mine." He rubs a hand down his face. "Soul mates are sacred, Kai. I've drilled that into your head since you were young, and what I accepted—even if Lucienne had made up her mind—was wrong. I should've fought harder. Made her see that breaking our bond was a mistake."

My father speaks up. "You had no choice but to accept." *Keep an open mind, my son.*

I ignore his mindlink, keeping my eyes on the man I've looked up to all my life. He's always been there: he helped me shift for the first time, taught me how to hunt in my fur skin, and how to be a fair leader. While my father was a straightforward alpha, everything black and white, my grandfather saw that for every problem, there are at the very least five different outcomes.

Points of view vary, the same way one truth can splinter into a thousand interpretations, depending on who's wielding it. Perspectives are personal, and even the people with the best intentions can make cruel mistakes.

"I still deserved to know the truth."

"You weren't meant to find out this way. Not like this," he says, voice calm but determined. "Not before I had a chance to speak with Lucienne."

That doesn't sit well with me. Not with me, or my wolf. Not one fucking bit.

"Are you fucking kidding me? You still have ties to the mermaid queen?"

"I do." Doesn't deny it. He's stating a fact. "Just not in the way you might think."

"What's that supposed to mean?" It comes out garbled, the angry growl of the alpha wolf, and both men share a look. My beast doesn't like that; his rumble in my chest is growing louder. He's raking my insides, digging into my ribcage. "You think I wasn't ready to discover my fate entwined with deceit? That the precious stone you passed down to your bloodline wasn't a blessing, but a cage you buried?"

My father exhales roughly, his eyes darting between his father and his son. "Kai, your grandfather did what he thought best at the time. For you and the pack. He didn't know if the gods—"

"The gods?" My voice is low, dangerous. "You worried more about their unjust wrath over your *mermaid's* choice, but failed to warn me I might be caught in the storm. That your hurt bond would lead to consequences that are impacting my fate and mate."

How could they not see that? How do they not understand that the stone was never a true gift?

"It was never my intention to hurt you, Kai." A flash of pain tugs at his features, the remembrance of a bond never completed, but it's gone just as quickly as it appeared. His jaw sets and shoulders square, but his voice doesn't hold the weight of the leader he once was. Now, there's sorrow and regret. "I acted to protect this pack and my family, ensuring you'd never have to live with the hole I've carried for over a century. My connection with Lucienne is small and sporadic, a trail of dreams that your grandmother understood because she, too, lived with a loss. I never dishonored her. I honored her every day of her life, and thank the gods for granting me a second chance at love. But Lucienne…" His throat bobs, and he stops to clear it a few times. "She's a part of that past."

"She rejected you." My voice is venom-laced, but my chest tightens in a way I hate. Regret fills me, but there's too much anger in me to take it back.

"She protected me and mine," he spits out from between clenched teeth, his wolf rising behind dark eyes—the same chocolate tone as all the males in my bloodline—and had he not been my grandfather and someone I love, I would've knocked his fangs into the back of his skull. "Her choices hurt her more than they hurt me, Kai."

I cut him off with a scoff. "What I see and understand is that you've betrayed me. That your secrecy—defending *her*—might've cost me my mate. That while I've been bleeding to provide for our people and keeping us safe, you've forgotten where your loyalties lie."

"You think I wanted this? That I didn't beg her to reconsider, to not walk away from me?" It leaves him on a snarl, and my wolf answers. I bare my teeth and take a step forward. There's only so much my beast can take, and being away from his mate isn't helping.

It's the opposite.

Nerissa is a craving I can't ignore or deny; she's burrowed deep under my skin, fusing with my marrow, a part of every breath I take.

"All this rage and guilt will tear this pack apart if you don't get a hold of yourselves." My father's voice cuts through the tension, and my head snaps toward him. Julius steps forward, his shoulders tense but steady, and places two hands on the table. Leans forward. "You are kin, not enemies, and need to stop being defensive. My son, you have every right to demand answers, but unless you truly listen, the point is moot. And you..." his eyes narrow on his father "...stop defending Queen Lucienne and start explaining. Your alpha doesn't need the tragic love story, but the promises made and possibilities you dreaded. It's time. No more hiding."

For a few minutes, no one speaks. The only sound inside the stone chamber comes from the rustling wind through crevices and the flickering flames.

"You're blindness to the real issues is what cuts me the deepest," I say, voice low, but the edge of ire I'm teetering on slips through each syllable. Veris, who's been quiet this entire time, speaks through our private link. ***Torren's waiting for us outside the underground cells.*** I give him a small nod and instructions. ***Head on over. I'll meet you there in ten.*** "I can understand everything but not telling me that Nerissa Del Mare being my mate was always a possibility. For as long as I can remember, the mermen have tried to steal the stone. They've attacked our ships, treated us like enemies, and have shown they have little to no honor—yet I'm tied to the heir to their throne, and I'm expected to smile about it."

"Kai—"

"No, Father." I give them my back as Veris exits, and it's meant to drive the point home. I'm beyond disappointed; my respect for my grandfather is hanging by a thread. "At any point in the last fifteen years, he could've approached me and explained. The mess created by King Atlas and Queen Lucienne's selfishness is more than far-reaching. My mate helped the mermen army steal the very gift her grandmother donated as a gesture of what—pity?"

"You know why." That's all my grandfather says, but he does stand up from his seat. The chair scrapes harshly against the ground; I still don't turn around. "The stone was meant to be a guide, so that no Daire wolf would experience what I did. Lived through. You're grandmother softened the pain, Kai, but the ache never faded."

"And yet they've spent years trying to reclaim that precious gift." I turn to leave, then, and make it as far as the doorway before I look at them from over my shoulder. "They've made us the enemy, and now, I might lose the very thing you tried to protect me from."

"She's dying." Not what I expected, but it's the truth. I see it in his expression. "Her bond with Atlas has kept her alive, but the longer we go without any contact, Lucienne wastes away."

"And will the stone save her?"

"No."

"Then why use my mate to reclaim it?"

"Not them, Kai. Atlas wants it."

"That's even worse." With that, I walk out, fury and worry beating in time with every step. I don't believe in coincidences, and rogues appearing in San Tico on the night of the challenges—where I scented her for the first time—doesn't sit well with me.

If they know something, I'll find out. Even if it means ripping it from them a bone at a time, because I'll never stop fighting for what is mine. And Nerissa is just that.

My mate. My home.

THE AIR down in the underground cells is damp, heavy with body odor and fear. The latter of which is heaviest, especially for three wolves who'd been wearing scent blockers the last time they'd been in my presence.

They thought they'd been clever.

That they could cheat me.

Torren and his brother are standing just inside the iron door, leaning against the wall, but they straighten when they sense me. Both nod, their hulking forms half-hidden by shadows, but it's the glint of metal that catches my attention. It's my sword in Otto's hand, that and the leather scabbard.

"How?" I ask, but it comes out edged with steel.

Otto flinches, but fights himself while keeping his neck bared. "The blacksmith delivered it last night. Said it was sharpened and balanced; he didn't want to disturb you, Alpha."

"Thank you." Taking it from his extended hands, I run a finger down the sharp blade before wrapping my fingers around the handle. I test the weight and balance, twisting it to see how it feels. A slow swish cuts through the air, clean and precise, as three rogue wolves are brought to their knees before me.

Filthy. Fearful.

The first to the left is a male with the intelligence of a potato. No pack wolf or rogue would bare his teeth at an alpha wolf, especially one who looks as if a strong breeze will knock him over.

That bravado will not save him.

"You reek of piss and fear," I murmur, crouching low while tilting my head to the side. He's easily sixty pounds less than me with no muscle mass or weapon, and I pity the idiot. "You're also too stupid to realize you're already dead."

He laughs at that, the sound ugly, a hint of panic in it. "I'm not afraid to die, but you should be."

"Is that so?" I bring the tip of the sword to his ear and saw back and forth slowly. The skin flays easily, as if it were butter, and I make a mental note to send the blacksmith a gift in appreciation. "Tell me more."

"We're not afraid of you," he spits out, fighting back the urge to flinch away. What's left of his ear will fall to the floor with two more glides of my blade.

"Sure."

"Spiro had a powerful backer. She'll protect us." *She. Interesting.*

"What else?" The cartilage is hanging by the thinnest thread as blood spurts and seeps from the wound. Nothing big or traumatic, just small increments that bring a smile to my face. After the last few days, I need an outlet, and this fool is the perfect target. "Don't be shy."

"The mer—"

Gagging behind us cuts him off, and I look over, finding the female retching, deep, painful heaves with little to nothing coming out, and I give Veris a look.

Get her water and a chair.

He doesn't respond, but I hear him exit the room and return a few minutes later. The scrape of metal is loud as he drags the seat over, and I raise a brow. Veris shrugs, but he's gentler when handing the woman a paper towel and an unopened water bottle.

She's grateful for both, whispering an almost too low to hear *thank you* while the other male shows me his marked neck. Same one she has. A sign of respect from two rogues, I could easily kill within these walls, and no one would bat an eye.

The punishment for trespassing is death. And yet, nothing pleases me more than the look of utter disgust on their companion's face. He's angry. Disgusted. Jealous. It all pours from him, mixing with his already putrid scent—the combination tickles my nose.

It also amuses me, and after the last few days I've had, it's appreciated. Makes me feel warm inside. And in the spirit of being a good host, I make a few decisions.

"Veris, get these two moved across from him and into a clean cell. I want them fed, offered a shower, and given a mattress and blanket to lie on." Once my beta leaves to do what I need, I give the final pull of my sword, severing the assholes ear completely off. It lands near his knee after a bit of bouncing, earning me a glare. Pitiful as it is. "Is there a problem?"

ALPHA
KAI

FIFTEEN

I dreamt of her last night.

Sad. Miserable. My siren called out to me, her voice cracking like delicate glass.

Something was causing her pain, and each cry tore through my chest, leaving a gaping gash behind. Her pain was mine, and I felt it as if I were receiving a thousand lashes and each one was dipped in acid.

I wanted to touch her. Soothe her.

Nerissa was there, just a few strokes from me—her hair fanned out like an inky black halo while her tail flickered in the prettiest shades of purples, blues, and soft touches of pink.

My beautiful, sad mermaid.

I swam toward her. My muscles were burning, arms tearing through the current with everything I had, and yet it wasn't enough. Because no matter how fast or hard I pushed myself, she was just out of reach.

Slipping further away.

Drifting into the shadows.

Leaving me.

I'd woken up drenched in sweat, my chest heaving and cock throbbing in time with my rapid heartbeat. The swollen head was sensitive, dragging across the cotton sheet with each jerk and leaving smears of pre-come as proof of my need.

There's no peace in it, either.

I'm still hard, missing her and haunted by the unshed tears in her eyes before the sea cloaked its princess.

"I'm going to find you, little treasure. I'll bring you home," I groan to the empty room, cursing that fucking stone again. It was never a gift, but an empty tether.

Dragging myself from the bed, I stalk into my bathroom. Restless fury is riding me; I'm leaving soon, but each tick of the clock feels like an eternity, and the separation aches in my bones. Mates aren't supposed to be without the other for long, especially newfound ones. I brace my hands on the counter, head hanging low as I force air into my lungs. Inhale. Exhale. Inhale.

A deep rumble escapes my chest, and I look up, catching my reflection. I'm more beast than man: eyes a honeyed gold, hair damp with sweat, and muscles twitching with the restraint to hold him back.

And then I caught it.

Soft. Bright. Impossible.

Orange blossoms.

The scent slipped in like a blade, sharp and sweet and mine, slicing through me with precision. My head snaps toward the window, then I stumble toward it, shoving it wider. It's stronger now. The fragrance is unmistakable.

"Motherfuck," I groan out, my cock thickening to the point of pain when my eyes settle on four new bushes. They're new. In full bloom. White blossoms are vibrantly thriving under the early morning sun.

My villa had been built for her, for the day I'd find my mate.

Private. Secluded. No neighbors or interruption; my pack knows better than to trespass unless there's a dire emergency or death, and yet someone planted these, and it's a welcome surprise.

A low growl rumbles in my chest, cock dripping pre-come, and I rush out of the room. There's an outdoor shower I added a few years back, built for convenience after long hunts or filthy journeys. Easier for me to clean off without tracking blood or grime into the house—I also enjoy it.

The freedom. The open air.

Tonight, though, it feels like a blessed curse.

The partial wall around it covers from my upper body down to my shins, with the open side facing my new plants. My nose twitches, and I smile as the faint remnants of someone else's scent hit me. She also left a small shovel behind, one I gifted her a few years back with a floral handle.

I'll thank Mom later.

A breeze sweeps my backyard, erasing the last traces of Mom's marker while enveloping me in Nerissa's as I turn the shower on. Immediately, I'm hit with cold water hammering my skin, but it does nothing to cool me. My hands brace against the wall, water cascading down my heated flesh, and yet she clings to me.

My siren. My mate.

"The gods are playing with me," I hiss from between clenched teeth, and her scent thickens as if they agree. She's burrowing into my blood—I can almost taste her in the air—and my cock gives a harsh, painful jerk. My knot thickens as the sea-breeze melds with orange blossoms. "Fuck, I need her. That pretty little pussy wrapped around me tight."

My cock pulses again, thick and demanding, and I wrap my fist around it. A snark rips from my throat at the contact, not pleasure but fury. I want her hands on me, not my own, but my body betrays me. Needing. Aching. Need to sharp to ignore.

I stroke hard, each pump merciless like a punishment. My breaths are fast and teeth bared as I imagine her pinned beneath me, her mouth open, body trembling as I ride her hard and without pause.

I'm back to that night in the jungle, her body pinned beneath mine while those hooded, violet eyes watched me with desire. How she tightened her legs around my waist, her sharp nails broke my skin, and that heavenly cunt gripped me like a vice.

Tight. Pink. Heat.

"Son of a bitch." I come with a savage growl, my release spilling hot and thick in four sharp spurts. They land against the house wall, then slide down before disappearing into the grass below. My forehead slams against the arm holding me up, chest heaving, my breath nothing more than ragged bursts.

But even emptied, I still ache.

Nothing will truly satiate me but my mate. The pain in my still swollen knot is proof of that.

Forcing myself upright, I wash and rinse my body. I'm on autopilot, movements mechanical as I head back inside naked and dress myself in all black clothing.

I'm heading to an execution, and the blood in my veins has cooled to ice for now.

I'm coming for you.

The cells are quiet as I walk in a few minutes later. Torren and Veris are already there, my sword glinting from where I'd left it yesterday, hanging from a mount.

A reminder to the trio, a message visible from the cells they were moved into last night. From the very back to the front, just feet from the only door in or out. We're not that far from the sea, either. And if you strain just enough, you can hear the waves crashing against the rock formation on this side of the island.

Freedom is so close. A torture and tease.

Five pairs of eyes follow me, but I don't pay them any attention. Not yet. Instead, I take in Torren and the varying shades of yellow bruises along his arm. He's standing taller than yesterday, his face blank, but rage pours out of him. His encounter with the mermen general still bothers him, and I see the thirst for vengeance reflected back at me.

Is the wound closed? I ask through our link, needing to make sure he's fit to help me if needed. Not that I expect him to; rogues have never scared me. Not one, or ten, or fifty. They're weaker, smaller, and aren't properly trained—fail to meet me in hand-to-hand combat.

His response comes in the form of a short nod, patting the area to show he's okay. Veris doesn't say anything, but he does push forward a small rolling cart. One that I raise a brow to.

It's gold and ornate with a thick glass shelf on top and completely out of place for the royal pack's dungeons. *My mate said we could borrow it, but we'd better not break it. It's her tea cart.*

A snort escapes me, and three pairs of eyes widen; they don't know what to do with the laughing alpha wolf standing between their holding cells. To the left, a dead man is breathing—his body slumped against the back wall. Every rise and fall of his chest is a wasted gift from borrowed time.

His minutes are numbered, and my fingertips itch where my claws are hidden. I can almost feel the drip of his blood on them, the rich metallic scent filling the room and my wolf with the satisfaction of killing a useless, disgraced wolf.

To the right, there's a mated pair. Smaller in size, clearly omegas, and scared. They've showered, have clean clothes on, and appear less gaunt than yesterday. The faint traces of their meals linger in the stale air, meat and bread, and I smile at them. Not menacing, but to show I mean them no harm, unless...

Cooperation is the literal key to their survival.

Together, they huddle against the right wall beneath a blanket. Not for warmth as the cells aren't cold, but for comfort. Their scents, though, tickle my nose. The male and female are both drenched in fear and dread—the tiniest bit of hope—the weight of their emotions slamming into me.

Raw and impossible to ignore. I see every tremor and feel every unspoken plea.

I've had time to think since yesterday. To plan. To reconcile what I know with what reality shows.

And both begin and end with one person: Nerissa Del Mare. My pretty little siren.

If her plan had been to sentence rogues to their deaths, so be it. If she wanted me distracted, she accomplished just that. That much is clear, and so I'll treat them as such.

These two will not die—yet. The opportunity will be presented, but it's up to them to decide their own path.

"Good morning," I say, my voice carrying through the silence. The three don't answer; they only stare. Two with resignation, and one with defiance. The latter of which knows he's going to die by my hand, just not how—slow and painful, or fast and merciless.

My lips curl. "I said, 'Good morning.'"

The words crack against the stone and metal bars, echoing like the crack of a whip. Four heads bow at once—my beta, gamma, and the pair—while my insolent guest fights the urge. It's painful and stupid, the strain on his face causing the veins in his temples to pop and his eyes to become bloodshot. His entire body shakes, forcing him lower, and I give him a gentle push by unleashing my full command on him.

Within seconds, he's prostrated with his head to the ground and his shoulders bunching up to his ears. Shaking. Dragging in ragged breaths.

"Good morning, Alpha," a soft, feminine voice says at last, and I turn my head in the couple's direction. She's tiny for a she-wolf. Shy, too. Her mate, on the other hand, quickly drops his eyes, tension radiating from every pore. His fear isn't for himself—not entirely— but for her.

And that much, I can respect. Admire even.

Because now that I've found what's goddess-given mine, I understand. One's mate comes before all else, including one's life.

You breathe, live, and die for your fated mate. Their safety, their life, their place is at your side—it's what defines a good wolf.

Moreover, to have her in harm's way without a way to protect her is torture. A punishment I don't wish on anyone. Even my enemies.

"What's your name, young wolf?" I ask, voice softer yet tinged with anger. The way she flinches twists something in me, and the feeling further cements my plans with the couple.

"Brina," she whispers, shaking and clutching the blanket in her hands so tight her knuckles turn white. The male, for his part, wraps an arm around her shoulder, pulling her closer. His comfort helps settle Brina, and after a few deep breaths, her chin lifts a fraction of an inch before she meets my eyes. "My name is Brina Martin, and my mate is Jonathan Rolf."

I catch the quick squeeze of his fingers on her shoulder, the way she further leans on him, and then my nostrils flare. Today, they smell less like rogues and more like pack wolves. No distinct scent, but the putrid stench of a feral beast is almost gone. *They're not lost causes.*

Both Veris and Torren agree through our mindlink, their wolves giving low approving chuffs. They see what I do and approve of what's to come.

I'll allow them to live and thrive inside the royal pack.

Across the cell, the third rogue lets out a short, derisive laugh. It's dry and venomous, the sound scraping like claws on glass as he pushes himself up to a sitting position. Sweat drips from his face onto his tattered shirt, and he uses the hem to wipe it away. Not that it helps much; he's trying to hide his panic beneath an obnoxious false bravado.

"Something amusing, rogue?"

"It's touching," he replies, a sneer in his tone. He's speaking to me, and yet it's the defenseless woman he focuses on. "Little Brina is playing nicely with an unworthy alpha. Will you bow next or kneel at the feet of our king?"

Jonathan's head snaps up; the sounds coming from his chest are low and warning. "Watch your tongue, Levi."

"Or what? What the fuck can you do?" He stands on unsteady legs, almost crashing back down twice but manages to stumble to the cell's gate. There, Levi presses his face between the slats—squeezing and protruding—yet only serves to scrape his skin with the rusted metal. That, and get stuck. *Fucking idiot.*

I step forward, slow and deliberate. My boots echo on the stone, each thud punctuating the weight of my intent. There's violence on my face, the promise of pain, but he smiles at me. Lips curling back, his teeth flash a second before I reach him.

"Go on then, Alpha." Spittle leaves his dirty mouth, barely missing me. "Show these ungrateful pieces of shit just how much of a monster you really are."

My smile is slow. Dangerous. "With pleasure."

One second, he's standing with his face between the slats, and the next, there's a horrified look on his face. My claws are buried in his throat, eyes wide with disbelief as I grip his vertebrae and yank my arm back. I tear, ripping through sinew and cartilage—bone—until his throat comes undone and a free spray of crimson splatters across my front. The wet sound echoes, a final gurgle before silence.

Only then do I let him drop.

There's a heavy thud when I turn around, my wolf at the forefront watching them. "I wasn't going to waste another second listening to his drivel, but you two will talk." Jonathan has Brina pulled against him, shielding her as much as he can from the bloody scene, and their fear is heightened, as if I'll turn on them next. I shake my head. "You two are safe. No harm will come to you here, but I will need every bit of information you have on Spiro and his *backer.*"

They don't believe me, but they nod just the same.

"Understood, Alpha," they say in unison, but it's my mother I'm attuned to. She's just outside the entrance, a little impatient huff in her. Last night I stopped by my parents' home, and the moment she opened the door and looked at my face, she pulled me into a hug. No questions asked. No demands for me to forgive.

I know my father mindlinked her the moment I left the meeting. The man likes to gossip with her about everything, but right now she's just a mom and her pup. My being thirty-three means nothing to her; I'll always be the son she birthed, cared for, and helped become the man I am.

"I'll see you in my office in one hour. Gamma Torren will escort you." Looking at Torren, I give him a look he immediately understands without words. They don't go anywhere without him, especially while around other pack members.

With that, I turn and exit without bothering to wipe my face clean. She notices, stepping past me with a wrinkled nose and a low, *don't even think about it* when I try to give her a quick hug.

But then she stops and looks back over her shoulder at me, her face holding a mixture of pride and sadness. "Do what you must, my son." It's spoken softly, though the words carry the weight of command. The old luna of our pack is standing tall. "Talk, eat…do whatever you must, but come back to us. We'll be here to welcome you back."

"Thank you."

"Good." Mom winks at me. "Now go bring my pretty daughter-in-law home, Kai. Siren or not, she's your mate, and that makes her pack."

ALPHA KAI

SIXTEEN

J onathan arrives less than an hour later, clutching a steaming cup of coffee in his hand. His steps are slow and hesitant. The weight of my gaze is enough to make most wolves falter— and he does, right inside the threshold of my office. It takes a few seconds for him to right himself, to check that nothing was spilled, before he stops and waits for me to address him.

There's one thing missing, though. No mate.

She's nowhere to be seen, and I lean back in my chair, raising a brow at the man. "Where is she?"

"She's with your mother, Alpha. The old luna said she was too thin and looked too tired, and took it upon herself to cure both ailments," Torren answers for him, stepping inside with a quiet arrogance only my third can pull off. Veris has a bit of that in him, too.

It's part of the hierarchy. If I die, Veris would take over as I have no heirs, and Torren would have first rights to claim the beta position.

"Who's with them?" He's as protective of her as I am, having grown up with her as the mother of the pack. Lunas are important for more than being the alpha's mate and moral compass. She's a maternal figure to all, young and old, and brings comfort in times of unrest. She's unity personified, and not one member of this pack would ever put her life at risk.

"Your father took over watch duty, said he wanted to show the new member around. Show the pack they are welcome here."

A faint smirk tugs at my lips. Typical. My parents are social and very much involved—retirement has softened him—yet neither oversteps. My word is law, even with them.

"Fine." I shift my attention back to Jonathan, letting the silence stretch between us until he shifts. Only then do I wave to the chair across from me. "Sit. We have a lot to discuss."

Jonathan sets his coffee down carefully at the edge of my desk, hands trembling. "Alpha."

"Please sit." The words come out sharp, the command rolling from my chest. He obeys immediately, lowering himself into the chair opposite mine. A few times his eyes flicker to the only exit, but he only finds Torren.

My gamma stands with his arms crossed, large body leaning against the wall to the left of the closed door. He doesn't call him out on it, but rather tilts his head in my direction.

"I'm not a liar, Jonathan. If I said you're safe, then that's what you are."

At my words, he nods. Becomes a little less rigid, even. "Thank you."

"Don't thank me yet. How this ends depends solely on you."

"Okay."

"Tell me everything. Leave nothing out," I tell him, voice calm, yet the wolf comes through in the command, dangerous and unyielding. "From the beginning, what led you to Isle San Tico the night of the challenges? What were you after?"

"We didn't plan on it, Alpha Kai. Not at first." Jonathan swallows hard, throat bobbing, and he takes a hearty sip from his mug. He doesn't set it down this time, but rather clutches it like a lifeline. "This all started about a month ago, when Brina ran away with me. We're from neighboring small islands on the southern edge of the northern sea, near the capital city of Bazra."

"Are you from Liora or Selvora?"

"I'm from Selvora. It's definitely colder than Liora; nobody uses the beaches there."

"And you ran away because…" I had an idea, but I wanted to test just how honest he'd be. Mar de Marea Plateadas, or *Sea of Silver Tides,* is known for its archaic traditions. Some places, like its capital city of Bazra, have taken on a more modern approach to civilization, but it's the city of Morvane that controls its waters.

Morvane is a gothic port city on the northernmost point of Mar de Marea Plateadas. It's controlled by vampires, an older-than-dirt coven with money and a penchant to play with mated pairs. None of the members have found their beloved, and to them, a soulmate is nothing more than entertainment. They have a lot in common with King Atlas in that perspective; neither the vampires nor sirens in power think past political advancement or money.

"Because our parents had plans for us."

"Go on."

"Arranged marriages." Jonathan inhales deeply and then lets it out slowly. His shoulders also sag a bit. "Hers to a territory leader, while I was to step in and take care of my sister-in-law and nephews. My brother passed away last year during a herding run for the vampires. He'd collect the donors, make sure they were fed and clean, then transport them back to the harem's private sanctuary not far from Selvora. A quick trip, what should've taken a day at most, but the boat capsized, and we have no idea why."

"Survivors?"

"None."

My fingers drum once against the desk. "So you ran?"

"Yes." Jonathan glances down at his hand, knuckles white. A

small crack appears on the cup, linear and doesn't spill its contents. "We ended up in Avaria after a friend gave me safe passage on his ship. He's a transporter and was already on his way to drop off shipping supplies at the port." Another pause, and this time he smiles a bit. "Avaria is amazing. Tropical and warm, different from what we're used to, and the locals treated us kindly. It's also where we met Spiro…literally ran into him."

"When and where?"

"On our second night."

Torren clears his throat then, and I shift my gaze to his. "Brina is on her way here."

"Okay." Pushing my chair back, I walk toward my liquor cabinet near the window and pick up the bottle of dark rum. This one is locally made, rich with caramel and pineapple. The cork stopper pops right out, and I pour three fingers' worth into a glass. The first sip burns slow and deep, a smoky sweetness sliding across my tongue. The warmth spreads through my chest, then my limbs, and I close my eyes for a second.

With my back to them, I stay that way until there's a soft knock.

I hear the opening of a door, a low *hello*, and then the scraping of another chair across the hardwood floor. Brina's worry is palpable, but she keeps her composure. Another change in her, just like Jonathan, is their scents.

Now, it's a mix of him and her. Citrus and cinnamon.

No rogue in them. No stench.

Do you notice the change? Torren's voice comes through, his link filled with trepidation. Second-guessing, or maybe it's a lack of trust in the two, but I sense it too.

I don't think they were ever truly rogues.

How could they fake it? Another question, but like Torren, I don't have the answers yet. *Do you think she's a hybrid? Part witch?*

Immediately, my wolf rejects the notion. I do, too.

Hybrids are hard to detect, but they carry one shared marker: a small red birthmark on the inside of their wrists in the shape of a spiral. I looked when she accepted the bottle of water from Veris, noticing the first change in her scent.

No. Not a hybrid, but she's been wearing a very strong blocker. Turning, I walk back to my seat and face the two. "Continue."

Brina's brows furrow, but she remains quiet. Instead, she grips her mate's hand. The same hand that a few minutes ago had the coffee cup. "I'm confused—"

"I'm explaining how we got here." She says *Oh*, and that's it. Just sits relaxed and smiles at him. His mate is more relaxed than he is, and there's a touch more color in her cheeks, too. The look he gives her is besotted, and my chest squeezes tight. "He was running from a grouping of three houses when he slammed into me, both of us tumbling to the ground. Spiro was trying to steal something—running from someone, and we covered for him when an older woman came at us with a thick wooden broom."

"A mage?"

"Not sure, but she was angry," Brina jumps in, her eyes unfocused as if remembering that day. "It happened so fast, and we didn't want to get caught up in his mess, so we lied."

"The woman, she bought this?"

"I remember her looking at us, Alpha. Like almost seeing through us, and then she smiled. Just smiled, and bid us a goodnight."

"Then what?"

"Spiro took us in."

I arch a brow. "Took you in or used you?"

"Both." Jonathan grimaces, while Brina nods in agreement. "He and Levi—they were partners. One stole, the other kept lookout. My mate and I...we just tagged along. It was survival; were staying in the background until we saved enough to head east and buy land in one of the less-populated villages."

"And the mermaid?"

"How did you know she was a—"

"Answer me." This leaves me on a sharp bark, the command of my wolf. He's pushing for me to hurry this up, so I can leave and find our mate. He wants her found, mounted, and claimed with our bite mark adorning her pretty little neck. And I need that, too, but leaving without settling them or having the facts will only delay our hunt. "Where is she? What did she do?"

"S-She wasn't like the other homeowners on Port Avaria and caught Spiro stealing. Literally had his hands on some coral-carved jewelry box, and glamoured him. Then Levi."

"Not you or Brina?"

"No. The woman, whose name is Nerissa, left us alone. No explanation why, she just did."

"What did she say?"

Brina's expression is apologetic. "We don't want to anger you, Alpha. It wasn't nice."

"Say it. Don't sugarcoat a single word."

"That you weren't a true king. That wolves deserved better than a filthy, untrustworthy pirate and his kin." It hurts to hear, burns in my esophagus like the worst case of acid reflux. "She also wanted to know about a stone. Kept repeating something about a black gem and how important it was to find it. The reward she'd give Spiro for his help."

"Not you? Just Spiro?"

"And Levi," Jonathan adds. "Both were too eager to help, with Spiro thinking himself worthy of the crown."

"The guards on watch that night, too," his mate says, picking up the now lukewarm coffee her mate set down and takes a few sips. "She bent them to her will, got them to let us walk past without alerting anyone. Like we were invisible."

My claws scrape the desk. When they emerged? No clue. I'm too busy filing every single word away. Cataloging the betrayal of a centuries-old agreement between her grandmother and my grandfather.

He'd drilled it into my head since an early age. Our bloodline wouldn't swim in the sea, and the mermaids wouldn't sing for wolves.

A treaty Nerissa Del Mare broke.

My traitorous little siren.

"And the scent blockers?"

They share a look, but I catch how Jonathan pats her hand with his unoccupied one. How his body shifts toward her—support and comfort.

"I made it." Her voice is tinged with fear, yet underlined with optimism. "My father is a man of science, and I grew up around herbs and compounds—the territory leader keeps him well stocked. He's tested and tweaked that recipe for years, and a few years ago, perfected it. It gave him leverage in our pack, a way to move up the ladder by asking for a marriage alliance I didn't want. In the end, it helped us. Kept us hidden."

Before I could ask for further clarification, her mate leaned forward. Not much, but enough to pull my gaze to him. "Alpha, please know we didn't want this. We just wanted to be free and safe. It's why I played along with Levi that night, until he got pushy. While Spiro challenged you, he wanted us to create a diversion—use Brina to get the males riled up—but the attention I caught was that of your beta and gamma."

Tilting my head, I study the two. There's no malice or lies in their explanation. Instead, they look at me with hope.

"Do you want more than freedom? A home here?" They blink, and the excitement that builds brings a smile to their lips. Both nod quickly. "I'm giving you a chance for more. Pack, protection, and a future with your mate. Do not let me down. You'll be on probation, but will help where needed and earn my people's trust. Fail once, and I will personally kill you. Understood?"

"Yes, Alpha. Thank you." Again in unison, each signing their names on a contract I push across my desk before dismissing them. The other pack omegas will help them get set up in a home, then pull them into the chore rotation.

When I get back, I'll deal with the scent blocker and the issue it might provide in the future. For now, though, my thoughts head back to Nerissa. Her call tugs at me, even miles from sea.

I'm coming, pretty siren. And you'll have a lot to apologize for with that sinful mouth.

NERISSA

Seventeen

Fingers sweep up and down my back, getting lower with each pass. It feels so good, and I'm pulled from a deep sleep by the touch. The hand is strong and manly, the rough patches of skin from manual labor only adding to the erotic touch. More so when he digs those fingertips in deep, working on tense areas.

Because the last few days have been rough. My eyes ache from tears that don't fall. It's why mermaids sing their lament to the open, endless sky. We release our troubles, weep for those who died at sea, and bless the waters with our essence.

And yet, everything fades away when warm lips kiss the base of my spine. When the scent of Guaiac wood and pineapples wraps around me. "Open those pretty eyes for me, little treasure."

My lashes flutter open, my mind slow to process, but there he is. My Kai. My mate. It's impossible. I know this is a dream, and yet a smile curves at my lips. "Hello, Alpha."

"Sweet Nerissa." His voice is tough and guttural, his wolf

watching me through his human eyes, and I shiver. I'm happy and relieved, but then sadness slams into me from all sides. So much has happened, and I'm free-falling into an abyss that scares me.

"No, sweetheart. Don't cry." This command is laced with patience, and for some reason, it only makes me feel worse. "Tell me what's wrong."

"Everything, Wolf. Every freaking thing." I let out a shuddering breath as the sky breaks with a torrential downpour. It's violent and strong, whipping against the outside of my home in Avaria. How did I end up here? Before I can ask him just that, lightning strikes right outside my window, and I jump.

It surprises me.

My emotions have always affected the weather. Rain when I'm sad and sunny skies when I'm happy—a soft golden pink when I'm calm. Yet this feels different. More.

"Then let me in. Let me shoulder what's made your heart heavy." He leans down and nips my shoulder this time. "Let me soothe your ache and heart."

"Can you make me forget? Just for a little while."

"I'll do and be anything you need, my female." A quick pull and the blanket over me disappears, cool air greeting my skin. I shiver, still upset, but then I'm met with the force of a spank that pushes everything but him from my mind.

His scent. His hand. His lips.

I'm attacked by all three as Kai climbs over me, his strong body hovering over me while he explores and kneads, landing a few spanks in between.

And each time, my hiss becomes a moan when it's followed by a nip to my shoulder. A kiss to my temple. The feel of those same fingers, my skin tingling from the strike, slipping between my thighs.

Spank. Stroke. Spank. Dip inside to the first knuckle and out again, dragging my slick from my clenching hole to rosebud to the swell of each heated cheek. Then again.

"Please, Kai," I moan, shivering when his hand lands at the curve where thigh meets cheek. The sting lashes, then spreads from my toes to clit, I'm one sensitive pulse. "Oh my Gods!"

"Not Gods, little treasure. I'm your alpha and mate. Yours." The next slap lands closer to my slick inner thighs before his fingers finally slip inside. First one and then two, stroking in deep and hard while his palm massages my clit. "That's it. Let me feel that pretty little cunt make a mess for me."

Lips drag across my shoulders, back and forth, leaving painful bites in between each peck. It's a delicious contrast to the pleasure rising, and I whine for him.

That sound does something to him. From sexy to feral, and I'm pulled up by the waist onto my knees, spread wide with his mouth on my pussy before I can scream.

Alpha Kai Daire eats me like a man possessed, his lips sucking on my clit while his fangs drop and a pleasurable sting takes me under. I come for him while he growls, the taste of me and my blood driving his wolf to a near frenzy. I can't do anything but accept.

I shake. I cry. I plead.

"One more, little treasure. Come for me again before I put you to bed."

"Oh fuck," It leaves me on a hiss when he nips my mound, paying extra attention to the sensitive flesh on either side of my clit. "Kai, please."

My whimper is rewarded by his thumb tracing from my entrance to my rosebud, adding pressure against my untouched hole. And the second he slips just the tip of his finger inside, I'm slammed headfirst into another orgasm.

My body sags as small aftershocks course through me; I'm a mess. Sweaty and slick and satiated—my alpha mate likes it, if his rumbling purr is anything to go by. I'm surprised when he doesn't use me to slake his need after, and instead, I'm shifted so he can lie beside me.

I'm engulfed in the warmest, most comforting hug. Kai's arms fold around me, warm and heavy, with his chest pressed against my back. "Better?"

I nod, because it's the truth. For the moment, I feel like I can breathe again. The proof of that is the pale blue sky outside my window, the edges of darker clouds creeping along the horizon. The sight is almost poetic. Like my emotions have temporarily calmed, but the storm lingers.

Just hangs there. Waiting.

Turning in his arms, I lay my head near his heart and listen to its beat. The sound is soothing, and I give myself permission to enjoy the reprieve because it won't last. "Thank you."

"Never thank me for taking care of you. That's a privilege, my mate."

"And to think I spent so many years hating you." At that, he made an annoyed sound from the back of his throat, the sound not entirely human. "Don't be mad at me, Wolf. I'm overwhelmed as it is and—"

"We'll deal with that another day, Nerissa, and I will revisit this conversation in person, but right now, I want to know what made you cry. Why are you sad, little treasure?" A flash of lightning, five seconds pass, and the ground beneath my home shakes. Anger and grief are overwhelming on their own, but together they wreak havoc on you. And that's how I feel all over again. Run down and strung out—the rush of anguish crashes into me, and my tears fall onto his chest. My earlier orgasms are nothing but a pleasant memory, even if my thighs are still slick and my pussy a little sore. "Tell me. Let me be who you lean on."

"It's my father." The words leave me on a low, choked whisper. "He was poisoned and has been unresponsive for days. Since the day after I left you."

"I'm sorry, sweetheart." Tight, he pulled me impossibly closer, his lips pressed against the crown of my head. "How did it happen? What have your doctors said?"

"The sea witch says it's not a toxin she's familiar with. Not from our waters or neighboring lands, but she's reached out to others and is praying for good news soon. We're hoping one of her connections knows—"

My eyes fly open, and I'm disoriented and confused for a second time. I'm not in my room in Avaria, and a warm wolf is definitely not beside me. Warm currents surround me, a gentle sway to them that helped me sleep and I look around, finding I'm in my father's room.

"Gods, how tired do you need to be to have a dream within a dream?"

Surprised, I stand up and find I'm a little dizzy. Don't remember how I got here, but then there's another slam of something, like a strike of solid on stone.

The vibrations travel, creating a painful pulse that I flinch from. There are also voices, two of them, but I can't discern what they're saying.

Leaving the bed, I creep closer, keeping close to the wall. One male. One female. And I'm surprised by the latter.

"This is getting out of hand, Orion. You said no one would get hurt." I'd expect some sadness in her tone, but all I hear is exasperation. Annoyance. She sounds nothing like my best friend.

"Do not question me, female. I do what must be done—she slept with that *mutt*. Gave him what should've been mine as her future king."

The next sharp sound echoes like a smack.

"Am I not enough? I'm your—"

"I'll forgive you this one time, but know your place, Naia. Never question me again. Don't insinuate you're worth more when we both know you're here to serve a purpose and nothing else."

"As your personal assistant, or plaything?" Naia hisses at him, but I can hear the hurt. The utter betrayal.

What is she to him?

"You, my pretty little toy, are whatever I want you to be. So play your role, smile politely, and bend over when I need you to." His tone is pompous and arrogant, almost challenging her to deny him. "Now go see if Nerissa is up yet. Maybe if she isn't, we can..."

He trails off, and a moan—hers—greets my ears. The sound of kissing follows shortly after. I'm disgusted and fuming, but glide back toward the bed and lie down, my tail half-covered by sea-silk. My eyes close, and I will my breathing to calm, just the occasional bubble slipping out.

I feel her presence a few minutes later. Naia doesn't say anything, but lingers while testing how deeply I sleep. First, by calling my name in a low voice and waving her hand in front of my face, then by giving me a gentle nudge. Nothing hard, but enough that if I were coming to, I'd snap my eyes open and see my best friend there. Not suspicious, with how many times she's stayed over in my room for days on end.

This time, though, I'm a statue and refuse to move.

Unmovable. Unshakable.

And after a few minutes, the woman I once trusted wholeheartedly swims away, satisfied, but whispers a few words that change everything...

"Please forgive me, Neri, but he's my mate."

I'M BACK inside my father's room an hour later.

I don't speak to anyone or stop to visit with grandfather or grandmother—I distrust everyone right now. From the stone, to the lies, to the whispers, I feel surrounded by a family I no longer recognize.

My reality is different from the stories shared among mermaids.

The problem is, I'm not one hundred percent sure who it benefits more...

Our king, who's tried to call me into the throne room a few times over the last few days, needing to discuss what happened and have me hand over his wife's magic. Or said queen, who comes to visit my father every day with a sad look on her face, as if she saw this coming and couldn't intervene.

I've thought about that, too. Took me a while inside this solitude, watching my father's unconscious body getting weaker, for it to hit me.

I sent you to the surface for a reason, not to reclaim my gift to Ephraim.

Those words hit differently when you've had a few days of silence with nothing but your thoughts to guide you. I've dissected conversations, come up with theories...

Please forgive me, Neri, but he's my mate.

Lifting my hand to the chain around my neck, I enclose the stone in my grip. It's cold, yet there's a faint comforting pulse that reminds me of my dream. The peace his heart beating beneath my ear brought me while Kai's strong arms wrapped around me tight.

Was I truly wrong about him?

"But why would he lie to me?"

"Because what he wants is to cure his own sickness." My head snaps toward the entryway, and I find my grandmother there. She's looking a bit stronger today, there's more color on her cheeks, and I see no tremor in her hand. "I'll explain later, but right now we don't have time to waste. You need to leave—"

"What the hell is going on?" I demand, my eyes narrowing on her. "Why do you look so..."

At my trail off, Queen Lucienne smiles. Her face is soft. "I had a dream last night, my child. One that literally breathed life back into me."

"You had a dream?" The implications are there, and I don't know how to feel about it. My dream was anything but innocent. *Did she...? Who did she...?*

"I did," she says as if I'd spoken out loud, head tilting to the side as she appraises me. "Much like you did, but judging by the blush on your face, mine wasn't on the same level."

"Grandmother, I truly do not understand."

"You shared a dream with your mate, Nerissa. In your despair, you called out to him, and the alpha replied. But more importantly, you welcomed him into your space." Her delicate finger taps mine, still wrapped around the stone. "Unconsciously, you sought refuge where you knew you'd be safe. With the one person in this world who will never hurt you."

NERISSA

Eighteen

T he care unit hums with quiet energy, shells glowing softly along the walls as the healers work in nearby chambers. My father lies in his bed, pale and his chest rising slowly in a shallow rhythm, while I stay by his side, gripping the edge of the bed until my fingers ache.

I'm still shaken from Grandma's warning. I'm still lost and uncertain—need the truth now more than ever, but I'm not given the opportunity to ask or demand it. Instead, I'm told to stop and listen while she sits close and her voice drops lower.

The one person in this world who will never hurt you.

"Push the red button on the wall, Nerissa. The small one." I do as asked, and immediately, a low sonar sound fills the room. It makes it hard to understand the noises outside in the hall and other rooms, and then I get it. For privacy. "Come close and pay attention. We only have a little bit of time before someone comes in and shuts it off."

"What's going on?"

Her hand finds mine, tugging me closer, and then she squeezes in a way meant to be comforting. "Your grandfather, sweetheart...he committed a crime he will never atone for. He's dying, Nerissa. Dying slowly, but his wasting away is unlike mine. I'll survive with proper care, while he has no cure."

"Proper care? What do you mean?" A deep pang hits me in the chest, and my eyes become glossy. "What did he do?

Because if he's responsible for my dad's poisoning...

"Your grandfather killed his mate." Her lips flatten and her tone is acerbic, pure disgust dripping through each word. "All for greed. To claim my throne, and my father helped him."

I stumble back, the shock causing me to recoil, but the question still slips from me. "Who? Was she a part of our—"

Grandma is shaking her head before I can finish, eyes softening for a split second before flashing with fury. "No. Not a mermaid."

"Then who?" A whisper. A plea.

"She was an orphan protected by an ancient vampire house in the north. The elder, Lord Severus, had taken the child in and fancied himself a godfather. Doting when earned and then expectant as she grew older. She became his right hand, wanted for nothing but handled everything from financials to finding suitable donors."

"And she agreed."

"He treated her like family, Nerissa. Let no harm come to her, and expected all vampires to protect her just the same." Grandmother stops, her brows furrow in thought. "In fact, they say the cruelest Lord Severus ever was to Angelis was when he found out she was mated to Atlas, and even then, his displeasure was expressed in softly spoken words."

"Why? Why would Grandpa do this?" I'm having a hard time reconciling the man who killed his mate to the man I've grown up with. Yes, he can be overbearing and a little sexist, but to actually take your mate's life is unforgivable. A slap in the face to the gods. "I'm—"

"It gets worse."

"How?"

Queen Lucienne swallows hard, her face so sad, the betrayal she feels coiling around us. "My husband killed his fated mate and married me, because he thought it would give him unchallenged power. Instead, it's tethered him to a slow decay triggered by a vampire's kiss."

Wait. What the hell? "Why would he drink tainted blood?"

"Not by choice." This makes her smile, slow and wry. "It was a peace offering made after, and Severus laced his drink. "Grandma shrugs. "Atlas had it coming, and now clings to the vampires in hopes of freeing himself. He always suspected Kai would be your mate and spoke ill of the wolves, just like he blamed your father's poisoning on the Daire pack. Mermaids have been whispering for days, offering well wishes to Marin while cursing those who left him face down on the shores of an abandoned island between San Tico and Avaria."

"That's not what happened!" I shout, and then bite back the rest of my retort. Drawing attention to us will tie my hands again. I need answers, not chains. "I'm sorry."

"Stop," a voice says from the bed, and I whip around to face my father. He's wincing a bit, face scrunched up, but holds a shaky hand up to me. I bypass it and bend to place my forehead on his.

"Thank the Gods you're awake."

"I'm okay, Princess. Promise." His eyes leave mine and focus on the person behind me. "Did you make the call?"

Rage coils in my gut. My disappointment is a bitter ache to swallow.

My father looks fragile, pallid against the low lighting, and yet people I trusted are busy bending the truth. I have to wonder just how deep Naia's betrayal goes. *Would she harm my family to please her mate?*

I'm pulled from my thoughts by Grandma's throat clearing. "I did."

"How far out now?"

"A few hours. Reinforcement will be stationed nearby if needed." She stands and moves to the other side of the bed and then leans closer, voice drops an octave or two. "Other things have changed since we last spoke, too. They want more, Marin. The vampires will use us—our waters—to move their blood herds, wealth, and weapons. And when the time comes, they'll use all three to strike San Tico. Kill every wolf on that island."

The words slice through me, and I gasp. "No." The stone in my hand remains black, but it's hot to the touch, and I'm singed by it. Not that I care. My mind and heart are screaming with dread. "*No. That...they can't!*"

"I'm sorry." Grabbing something from her pocket, Grandma presses it into my unoccupied hand. Her face is tight, almost haunted. "This is why you must leave tonight. Take the stone and hide it before your grandfather finds out."

Tears sting my eyes. "I can't leave you. I can't leave my father."

A tough cough breaks the silence. My father shifts weakly, his voice hoarse but steady. "Go, Nerissa. Your uncle and aunt are on their way; they know the truth and will care for me. We'll be fine, but you..."

"I won't be," I finish for him.

Grandma glances at the door; fins are brushing the current and coming closer. The sound is faint, a little distorted, but unmistakable. After a beat of silence, she meets my eyes again—hers blank now, just like my father is lying back with his eyes closed—as if this conversation never happened. "Do as he says, child. Run now, before it's too late."

THE PALACE FADES BEHIND ME, its polished grandeur and hidden dangers swallowed by the distance as I swim hard through the outer currents. My lungs burn, fin propelling me through the water. Every fast heartbeat is a reminder that I cannot go back. Every bit of the distance between me and the place I called home all my life hurts, but I don't slow down.

Not after everything I heard.

Because the people I trusted—who I still care for—decided their greed outweighs common decency. That the end justifies the means, no matter who gets harmed.

Up ahead, I hide behind a grouping of pillars. They're large enough to hide me as a guard on duty glides past me, spear in hand. His fins cut through the water silently, and my stomach twists.

Shit. I press myself closer to the stone, letting my cloak shimmer and bend the light, obscuring my outline. The merman slows, eyes narrowing, trying to find a scent or heartbeat—he can sense someone is there—before moving along while shaking his head.

I let out the shaky breath I didn't realize I'd been holding, my hand gripping the stone to find an anchor. For a few minutes, I don't move just in case, but then take a quick peek. Nothing to the left or right, and I push off the stone, swimming faster than I ever have before.

"Swim, Nerissa. Keep moving," I mutter under my breath, cutting through the current without pause until I break through the surface near Port Avaria. It's already dark out, the distant lights from various businesses creating a fractured light across the water. The scents of herbs and food—alcohol from the tavern—are sharp in my nose, and I sneeze. "Definitely different from the early afternoon hours."

My eyes don't sting; the sights in front of me are sharp as I walk up the beach and head toward my private cottage. The sound of laughter coming from the town's center—the late-night crowd from the ports, or those taking refuge for the night—carries through the wind.

I keep quiet so as not to attract attention. Hold my cloak tight as I slip through narrow back lanes, taking a shortcut through the outskirts, until I walk up my lit pathway. Only then do I let myself relax a little bit.

Not much, but enough not to jump at every single sound.

Once inside, though, I'm quick to pack, collecting the things I can't leave behind just in case. The book Magda gave me, jewelry passed down to me with certain protection spells, and a piece of Kai's pants I'd saved from that night. I'd found it in my bathroom after he left, just a small square that must've been dragged into the house in our haste, and still carries his scent.

Thicker, as a few drops of dried come had landed on it.

Guaiac wood. Pineapple. Leather.

I inhale deep and then shove it in the bag, making sure to close it quickly so I'm not tempted to rub the piece of fabric against my neck. Scent marking me the way he did that night, his skin against mine, his exhales warming my flesh until he'd been satisfied, and only then did he allow me more than an hour of sleep.

"No time for this. Pack and go," I remind myself, rushing back out the way I came after grabbing three simple changes of clothes and money stashed for emergencies. A few pieces of solid gold, too, just in case.

Nothing too big, but the bag weighed enough that I looked like a seasoned traveler heading to a new adventure while carrying everything she could need for any possible scenario.

It's less conspicuous this way. Creatures ask too many questions when they can't rationalize something.

The path from the house to the port is narrow, and I'm trying to catch one of the boats heading toward the western sea. Avaria's port is open all night, mostly because crews drink and then pass out onboard their boats, but a few like to make nighttime travel a commodity.

Moreover, I'm close to the fork in the road when it hits me.

His scent. Raw. Wild. Pulling against my chest, twisting this invisible tether, making my pulse hammer. My reaction is automatic, and I freeze, eyes frantically searching until I find the man staring back at me.

Gold meets violet, and the world stops. Then tilts. The call from his end of the semi-formed bond slams into me as though it were a tidal wave. I stumble, dig my feet into the sand-washed tar before righting myself—

I don't look away. Can't.

His form shudders violently, bones snapping and muscles twisting as black fur erupts along his tanned skin. It happens so fast. Painful as it looks, I blink, and the man I know is gone, replaced by a massive wolf the color of midnight. The wolf's shoulders ripple with power while his paws, huge and powerful, slam into the grass on his way to me.

I feel the earth tremble beneath my feet.

Run, dammit. Run.

I curse under my breath, spinning on my heel while my bag swings on my hip. My cloak snaps around me, a whisper of protection and concealment, as every nerve screams to go back. But I can't. If they found me last time, they'll easily find me again, and the last thing I want to do is bring a war to my mate's doorsteps.

The one person in this world who will never hurt you.

Before I left, Grandma pulled me into a tight hug before whispering something low, so only I could hear. She was adamant that I pick up Magda's book and read chapters five through seven and use it to my advantage during my travels. That I'd understand dream walking and shared sleep—how to help my wolf through it and guide him to me under the cover of the moon.

You will need each other, my child. Lean on the bond. Don't push it away.

"Goddess, please don't let this be a mistake."

Up ahead, the pier appears, and I push my legs faster. He's gaining on me, can almost feel his heated breath on my skin, but then I'm diving for the dark waves below, letting the cool waters swallow me. Beneath the surface, I kick hard, propelling myself far from

Avaria. The wolf's growl follows, though—guttural and angry—the vibrations travelling through the sand and into the sea.

It's a promise. A mate's declaration to hunt me down and bring me home.

And all I can think is:

Please do, my wolf. In the meantime, I will find you in my dreams.

ALPHA KAI

NINETEEN

O ur eyes met, and my world paused as those gorgeous
violet eyes warned me:
She will be my downfall. She will be my solace.
My female. My siren.

That was two months ago.

Two gods-damned months since I last scented her. Since I
watched her slip from the pier back into the sea, faster than my wolf
could chase her. And while her abilities make me proud, I'm also
angry at her for allowing this distance between us.

I've followed whispers, false trails—locations I see in my dreams
when she deems me worthy. And there's no doubt in my mind it's
real. All of it.

From the very first one, where her tears broke my heart and I
soothed her with my kisses, tongue, and fingers. She came for me so
prettily. Gave herself without doubt or holding back, moaning her
submission to her male.

Still, she eludes me during waking hours. Haunts me every few nights.

Look for me where the stars burn brightest, Alpha Kai.

"I feel her close," I tell my wolf, standing at the helm as we enter *Mar de Noches Eternas,* or Sea of Eternal Night. The waters are calm today, as if expecting me, when they're known for their merciless tides and a vast stretch where stars burn bright even in the light of day.

Beautiful to most. To me, it's another reminder of the empty ache clawing through my chest because the sea keeps her secrets well.

The deck beneath my boots rocks gently as Torren shouts orders up ahead. The sails snap high above, stark black canvas straining against the wind. Ropes creak against metal, and crewmen bark, while twenty wolves-turned-pirates run lines and guide the vessel closer to shore.

They know their roles: trim the sails, guide the rudder, and keep the ropes tight against the gust while the ship beneath us groans, the timber expanding against the water.

Leaving the wheel, I walk to the rail and grip it tight, leaning forward. Ahead, there's a rocky coast, a nameless village unknown to most but protected by vampires. The oldest house, at that.

I bare my teeth. "Drop anchor."

The command rolls out, and my men move like wolves on a hunt —formation tight, working as one, following their alpha. A heavy clanking sound follows shortly after, then a loud crash as it rips through the deep blue waters here. Less black, and cooler. Not cold.

The chains rattle as it sinks, while smaller boats are being lowered. Half the crew will go, while the other preps for departure; I don't want to be here longer than necessary.

"You ready?" Torren asks, already climbing over the banister and positioning his body to climb down. Me? I don't answer.

I simply dive down and swim ashore while the ethnic sounds of oars follow me.

THEIR VILLAGE IS SILENT. Too quiet. Stone halls rise in neat rows, their arched windows open as billowy curtains flutter in the breeze.

A herd house looms at the center, its doors barred but inside low whispers greet my ears. No one is crying, but there is an argument going on between a male and female. Her fear permeates the air, while he's aggressive in his demands.

Rage flood my veins. *This is what they do.*

Take women and force them into becoming donors with the promise of opulence and wealth. Some are given that treatment with caveats, but many end up like this place.

They're packed full. The men in charge of transporting sometimes abusing the humans. Because that's what vampires traffic: defenseless human with no strength or protection against the filthy bloodsuckers.

Cage and bleeds. Herd and harvest.

My nose twitches as blood leaks through a crack. It's old and watered down, but the scent is unmistakably metallic.

I break the door with one brutal kick, and screams fill the afternoon air. Women and men, I find both bound by a thin rope and naked, while two caretakers use a water hose to clean them off.

"Get them out. All but these two," I growl out, and Torren moves fast, his sword breaking through the flimsy ties used. The humans scatter at my bark, dragging the weak and I point in the direction of the ship I'd spied earlier. The one used to take them north to Morvane. "Find out if any of the men know how to sail and load them up. Await instructions after."

"Yes, Alpha," they answer in unison, yet Torren stays beside me, His nostrils twitching. "You smell it?"

"I do. Human, but not."

"Find the source. Bring him or her back alive."

"Aye, Alpha." Through our link, I catch his laugh as he heads toward a solid red door at the back of the room. It's thick and marked with four distinct claw marks in the front...

Turning toward the shaking caretakers, I point at the door from over my shoulder. "Who's in there?"

They hesitate, lips trembling, but one steps forward. "Lord Severus forbids us from—"

He doesn't get to finish; I rip his throat out, and blood sprays hot across my arm and chest. It drips onto the floor, and the few hurrying out gasp, and the other caretaker becomes as still as a statue.

"Move," I growl, wiping the crimson streaks across my jaw. And they do. Gods, they hurry out as if on fire, while my friend, the still-alive keeper, pees himself. He knows and I know that he will not make it to sundown, and all he has left is to pray.

His lips move, reciting an ancient prayer for mercy in death, while Otto joins his brother in tearing through the solid wood door. It creaks, groaning under the force, while a few of my men begin to tear through everything in sight.

In the grand hall, tables can be heard being overturned and fabric ripping, the crash of heavy glass and boots crunching them into dust. Then the other rooms. From one building to the other, they trash everything in their path until what's left is in ruin, and then they loot.

My crewmen begin to drag heavy chests from the coven feeding rooms: silver, coins, solid gold bars, and trinkets. Then, there are the ledgers. I'm given a few to look over as I babysit the man at my feet, his legs too heavy to carry the burden of being scum.

Because I may be a pirate, a feral beast at times, but I'd never hurt a fucking innocent woman, man, or child. That's a line you simply do not cross.

After the last gold rimmed chalice is smashed and there is nothing else of value, I look at the pack member closest to me. "Burn it all to the ground."

And they do.

Using a bottle of rum I'd brought ashore; I take a sip and hand it over as an accelerant. Within minutes, flames leap high, licking the bright blue skies, smoke billowing in the cool breeze. Screams echo from fear, stones and wood crack, while the herd compound becomes an inferno.

No more blood money here.

And yet, it's still not enough. My chest heaves, and my claws ache as Nerissa's violet eyes haunt me. As I hear her sweet, sultry voice whisper against my chest, body strewn over mine in my dream a few nights ago.

Look for me where the stars burn brightest, Alpha Kai.

It also reminds me of the conversation I had with my mother before setting sail. Her soft and lined hand was trembling as she pressed it to my cheek.

"When will you be back, my son?" she asks, voice shaky though she tries to mask it. Wolves surround us, crowding the dock as they load my ships with supplies, the air thick with prayers whispered to the gods.

"When the stone is in my hands and my mate is by my side." There's no other choice, not that I've been given one. Mates belong together, and I won't rest until Nerissa is here. "I promise, I will be back and reclaim my throne."

"Good. Cause I don't want it. It's too boring for me, Alpha." Veris says, and I turn fast enough to catch the smirk on his face. He's carrying my sleeping goddaughter, using her cuteness as a shield. Ophelia is adorable in all her scrunched-up, old-lady-looking expressions. Especially the milk-drunk ones, I've been blessed to witness over the last three days.

Their worry is palpable, as if their love.

My family. My blood. What I fight for.

"I'll take care of everything here, Kai. Just come back safe."

"I will. I'll send word back soon enough." With a final hug to my mother, a kiss on the forehead to Ophelia, and pats on the back from Veris, I walk away. It's not lost on me that my father and grandfather are off licking their wounds; they'd already wished me well in private, and while our issues aren't solved, we'll work it out later. My

attention is solely on reclaiming what is mine, and as prior alphas, they understand more than most just how hard the impulses ride you.

To mate. To hunt. To bite.

I'll be following the brightest star. She'll guide me back, I promise.

I'd mind linked those words to my mother before my ships sailed...

"Alpha," Otto's voice drags me from watching the flames kiss the sky. "We found someone you need to see."

The same scent gets closer. Not human. Not creature.

I turn to face them as they drag a man into the light, bound at the wrist but standing strong. He's also tall. Bruised up, a little thin, but it's his scent that's odd. Can't quite pinpoint it.

"I'm a hybrid," he says, voice hoarse from disuse, silver eyes assessing me. There's a glint of unleashed violence in them, but I don't sense a threat.

Stepping closer, I tilt my head. "You live here?"

"No." He spits on the ground, blood dripping down his chin from a split lip. "I was caged here."

"By who?"

"The northern coven."

"Why?" What do they need from you?"

"My mate." That violence in his silver gaze has a name now. It's the same one in my eyes, and it's a pain I understand. *Abandonment.* Not done on purpose, but it's the result of an unattended bond.

"Where is she?" I ask, giving Torren the signal to release his bindings. He's freed a second later, stretching his arm out, testing the free motion after being bound for Gods knows how long.

When he speaks again, it's low. Anger palpable.

"Severus took my female for his private herd, used her, and I'll gut every last one of them until I get her back." His gaze on mine is unflinching, and at the same time, not disrespectful. "Are you headed north by any chance?"

A growl rumbles through my chest. Brave bastard.

"What's your name?"

"Maleth Sinclair."

I study him, weighing the steel in his voice, the determination to find his mate, and how he carries the hollow ache of her absence.

"Betray me, Maleth, and I'll feed your entrails to the predators below."

A smile curves at his split lip. "Fair enough."

"Good. Now go take care of your first job." I point in the direction of the crying caretaker. "Make sure he doesn't live much longer, then help set up the victims on the boat. They need to head east and stay east. The waters on this side of the world are about to get bloody."

ALPHA KAI

TWENTY

Four months.

The sea has turned colder, sharper, as though each wave is a reminder of how long I've hunted her shadow. Months of chasing the pull, an invisible tether that yanks at my chest, and it whispers *north*. Always fucking north.

My men sense it. The desperation is growing inside me.

With each passing day, I'm more irritable. My beast, their alpha, constantly growling inside my chest—a wolf's cry for his mate. The lament of an unfinished bond.

Torren's discipline keeps the crew on task, Otto's learned to keep the wheel steady with unshakeable discipline, and Maleth—the silver-eyed, silent, and ruthless hybrid—watches the horizon as if he expects the vampire coven to rise from the sea itself.

Everyone is on edge. Something feels off.

My pack members do their jobs without question, always vigilant, knowing that when their alpha hunts, they do too. That a safe crew gets home to their families and mates, if they have one.

Many don't. I prefer it that way.

Understand the damage it causes now more than ever.

Still, the emptiness gnaws at me. Between the western pack and the northern stronghold lies nothing but barren land, high peaks or flat jungles, while the winds coming off the frigid waters below bite like teeth. The western sea fades behind us as the northern waters claim their place.

Mar De Marea Plateadas is named correctly for that alone.

Cold. Desolate. And the further north you go, the air itself feels thinner and the daylight becomes weak.

Why would she come here?

The Liora Isle is just beyond the horizon, the last semi-warm settlement before the frigid cold truly hits. The island is mostly used by travelers and traders as a pitstop to shop or sell their items before heading back to warmer waters. Most of those who come here are from the west, work, or have permission from the vampires to settle here…except for my wolves.

They serve me, not the vampires, and it irks the pompous blood bags.

"We're going to check out the packs while we're here. I want a wellness check." My voice carries across the ship, and I get a low, affirmative howl from everyone in response. No sooner do they respond than we pass the far edge of Liora, and my nostrils flare. The wind shifts, and my chest tightens, breath caught in my throat because beneath the salt and pine trees that grow here, I smell her.

Nerissa.

My grip tightens on the gunwale until the wood groans, a few fibers splintering as my heart beats inside my chest like a war drum. Every beat is for her. My wolf rumbles in my chest, and he pushes forward—almost forces a shift, and I fight back to keep him aboard.

He's demanding I go find her. Now. She's ours.

"Alpha?" Otto calls from the helm, catching the look on my face.

"Dock here."

"Are you sure? We can tender…" he trails off when I bare my

teeth at him. "This is a perfect choice, Alpha. Great for an early evening search."

"Drop the anchor." The crew leaps into motion, sails snap, and ropes whip as they're tied, and the wheel turns hard. We begin to slow, heading closer to the pale sand beach.

I don't wait for the anchor to fully catch before I'm overboard, gliding through the water and coming up a few yards from the ship. Behind me, Torren and Maleth follow, walking up the shoreline and assessing the area, and finding no signs of life.

"Search the land," I order, voice steady. A stark contrast to how I feel inside, and I think they notice because each man steps back. "Torren, take Maleth and five others and go east. Visit the pack there, get a quick report on their living conditions and finances while you're at it." As I'm finishing, Otto and the rest of the crew walk up beside us. They didn't bring the boats, choosing instead to swim to shore. "Otto, you're heading west with the rest of the crew. Sweep every inch of the island, and do the same if wolves are living there. There shouldn't be, but just in case the pack expanded and didn't report it."

They disburse, and I breathe in deep. Then again.

My nostrils flare as the wind shifts again, and I follow the notes of orange blossom to another part of the beach. I pass a driftwood graveyard, a rocky cliff, and then a crop of trees. It separates one side from the other, not quite a mangrove, but thick enough that I have to find my way around, and the closer I am to the other side, the stronger her perfume gets.

"She's here." It's a lash across my senses before the snap of an electrical rope wraps around my chest, and it tugs me closer. I can't resist the pull, nor do I want to, because it will always lead me to her —*my beautiful siren.*

My mate. My female.

Another few steps, and I'm just past the cropping of palm trees when her scent intensifies. Fresh and sweet, but there's a touch of sultry overpowering her call. It's want and need—a song only I hear or can claim.

She's aching for me. Demanding I ease her storm…

"Kai." One word, and it's glorious on her tongue. My ears twitch, and a low growl builds inside my chest, the early evening breeze carrying her whimpers while my cock throbs. It's hard and pulsing, my knot expanding slowly with an ache so deep my knees almost buckle.

Yet I remain upright. Take my position, legs spread and back against the trunk as I watch her perform for me.

Because she senses me. Knows her beasts—man and wolf—are near.

Licking my lips, I take quick notice of the coppery taste of my blood and the sharp canine piercing through my flesh. Then there's the fur on my arms and the claws currently destroying my waistband, pricking my skin in my haste to undo the button and zipper.

I rip through both. Then my shirt.

There are a few cuts and the sting of the salty breeze, but I pay no mind as those violet eyes meet mine after so long. And in that look, I see my every desire looking back at me:

To belong. To savor. To bite.

Raw and untamed, the wolf bares his teeth at her while I stroke my cock from root to tip and down again. A move she follows, licking her lips while those supple thighs I yearn to mark spread wider.

Goddess help me, she's perfection.

Pink. Wet. Heat.

A velvet oasis that makes my mouth water, and more so when I hear just how slick she is. How ready for my knot she is.

The sound of her fingers sliding in and out that tight little hole has me unconsciously taking a step forward, and I grunt in approval, enjoying the way she arches for me. How her heavy breasts bounce a little with each gyration of her hips as she meets the fast pump of her slim fingers.

Through each stroke, those violet eyes never leave mine. Nerissa nearly vibrates at the sight of me under the moonlight, and I'm gifted with the slow shimmer of her scales as they rise under her soft skin. Blues, pinks, and a touch of purple throughout, and they seem to come alive as she rides her hand.

Another call. Her natural allure.

But the bond between us hums and whispers that this is only for me. No one else.

An acknowledgement that makes me throb with male pride as I watch my gift from the goddess come undone.

I match Nerissa's every stroke with a violent one of my own.

My growls intertwine with her moans, creating a beautiful cadence I'll carry for the rest of my life. This song is mine, tattooed in my heart and sacred to me.

"My wolf, I'm so close," Nerissa cries out, thighs trembling, and I fall to my knees. I don't make a sound, crawling toward my prize in my half-shift form while the hand stroking my cock continues its brutal strokes. I fuck my hand to the rapid rise and fall of her chest, leaving a trail of my pre-come in the sand below. Honey eyes on violet ones, I don't stop until my unoccupied clawed hand is gripping one thigh and my lips are a hair's breadth from her slick mess.

I breathe her in, and she stills.

I purr for her, and those soaked fingers slip out.

"Oh Gods," she moans, and I tsk with a raised brow. I'm watching her, and the view from my place between her thighs is what heaven means to me. It's the throne I'll worship until my last breath and will retake in the afterlife. "Please. I'm—"

"You only worship me, little treasure. Your alpha." And then I ruin us both as I lick her from clenching hole to throbbing clit, rebranding myself as her taste slides across every nerve ending. It's a part of me now. Who I am now. "Motherfucking sweet."

It's the only thing I can get past gritted teeth as the first rope of come shoots out and lands on the crease where ass and thigh meet, then down to the sand below. Then another. My mouth latches onto her pulsing cunt as I come, and it triggers her release. I treasure this orgasm through rough licks and soft nips with my fangs across her trembling bundle of nerves.

She collapses back, body thrumming with pleasure. Nerissa doesn't speak; her fingers do the talking as they trail up my chest and neck before her delicate fingers embed themselves in my hair. There, she pulls, the pleasantly painful shockwave settling on my dick, and I throb against her slick little cunt. Let her move me to her liking, and she wants me close.

Skin on skin. Completely covered by me.

My female is so tiny compared to me. My treasured doll.

"Kiss me, Kai." she breathes out, her soft tongue gliding across my left fang. "Please."

My lips slant over hers in a desperate kiss. It's a little messy with teeth grazing, tongues tangling, and I want more. More of her sweetness and the way she moans into me, nails dragging down my arm as she kisses me back just as hungrily. She gasps when my sharp fang breaks the skin of her bottom lip, fisting my hair to the point of pain, and I welcome the sting when her little mouth whines for me.

"Gods, I've missed feeling you close."

"Me, too." Another kiss, quick but just as powerful. It rocks me. "But, Alpha, we're going to need some clothes. I can't walk out of here naked—"

A growl rips from me at the thought of anyone seeing her like this. She's for my eyes only. "That won't happen. I'll find you something."

"Thank you." Wrapping her lithe legs around my waist, she taps my side, and I turn us around, leaving her astride my body. My cock is hard again, her small, clenching hole sliding up and down my length while she gyrates above me. *Goddess, she's beautiful.*

"My perfect mate. So clever by showing me the way." Something passes across her features, a sadness I don't like, but before I can ask, she guides herself down my length. Slowly, inch by fucking inch, until reaching my knot. "Careful, Nerissa. You try to take my knot, and I will mark you under this northern moon."

"And maybe one day soon, I'll let you…"

"Is that a date?"

"No. It's a promise." Nerissa lies down, hips moving in a circular motion, picking up the pace until her lips are panting against mine. "Under the stars of Mar de Sombras, I will accept you as my mate and take your knot, bearing your mark for the world to see. Just as you will wear mine."

Her words snap the last bit of restraint from me. A savage growl rips from me as I flip her beneath me, driving into her with brutal, claiming thrust. She gasps, but that quickly turns into a moan when my knot teases her entrance with each stroke, stretching her a little more each time.

It slips inside a little and her eyes roll back. My hand grips her neck and my female coats me in her slick.

"Mine." A truth no one can deny. I fuck her hard and fast, rewarding her loyalty and trust in me. To care for her. To cherish her. "That's it, pretty siren. Give me another one."

"Kai," she screams out, meeting me thrust for thrust. Her nails break the skin on my chest, leaving tiny trails of blood down my tattooed chest. That bite of pain is addictive, seductive, and I tighten my grip a little more on her neck.

And if the way her cunt tightens is an indicator, my female likes it. So much so that she nips my chin.

"Motherfuck, beautiful," I bellow, my release ripping from me in a violent, almost painful wave. My spend fills her to the brim, then overflows as she comes at the feel of me twitching inside her. Each clench milks me, our combined juices creating the most beautiful mess on this empty, sandy beach.

"That was much needed, Alpha Daire."

I can't help but snort at that, gathering her close before kissing her soft berry lips. "My pleasure, Miss Nerissa." Looking around, I take in the darkened sky and zero signs of life. "Did you know this place was deserted? I'm surprised no one's come to investigate all the noise."

"Oh, umm. Well…I kind of glamoured the people in the closest pack to steer clear of this area." She shrugs, hissing a little when I pull out. Pouts too. "Well, that's going to be sore tomorrow."

"I'll take care of you. Draw you a warm bath back on my ship and—"

Suddenly her weight shifts, and before I can react, she's rushing into the water. Her tail appears immediately, the fin peeking out of the deep blue sea, while those violet eyes watch me with a bit of sadness and hope. The latter of which makes me pause.

"What aren't you telling me, Nerissa?"

"Just that I'm sorry, but I will make my promise a reality."

"No. Come back, and let's talk this out. Whatever it is, I can help you."

Her lips curve at that. "You already are. Just don't stop dreaming."

With that, she dives beneath the small waves, rushing in my direction and splashing my feet before disappearing. She doesn't come back, but I'm left with a gift—my chain and stone. Lit a fiery blue and thrumming with magic, I pick it up and enclose it in my fist.

If she wants me to keep dreaming, I will. If she wants me to chase her to the ends of the earth, I will.

All my pretty little siren needs to worry about is how much trouble she'll be in when I catch her.

WHEN I FIND the men again after securing clothes from a shifter donation box and slipping the chain inside a pocket, they are standing with an older she-wolf outside her home. They're discussing something, and all I catch is *Severus* and *Morvane*. I'm distracted, my mind reeling since she left, picking apart Nerissa's words—that I didn't fully pick up on their conversation.

Torren is the first to spot me. "Alpha, Otto's already surveyed the east side, and it's all clear. No inhabitants."

"And what about the pack leader here? Have you spoken to him?"

"That's what I've been explaining to them, Alpha. Everyone but a few of the older generations is gone."

"Gone where?" I ask, keeping my tone soft so as not to scare her. In that moment, I push aside the problem with my mate bond and focus on the needs of these wolves. "Who took them?"

"The vampires came and took them back to Morvane, starting with the scholar's family. All but Brina, and no one knows where she is, were taken away." At her words, my eyes snap to my gamma. *Again, the vampires. This needs to end.*

We're ready for a fight, Alpha. Been itching for one. Otto asks the woman something, walking with her inside the abandoned home. The rest of the wolves look to me for directions.

"Prepare the ship to head home. We're going to war with those nasty bloodsuckers."

The men thump their chests with their closed fists, and a few howl to the moon while I make a promise to the goddess.

When this is over, I'll bring her home. I'll destroy whoever or whatever is keeping her from me.

NERISSA

Twenty One

It's been four months since I left him on that beach. Eight months since Kai's hands, his teeth—everything that makes me ache—left me trembling for the first time. Every day I relive that night, memorizing the curl of his lips and the feel of his skin on mine, the way the Cordis Lux burned bright for us, tying us together for life.

But I already knew that.

I was sure of my ties to him the very first time I scented him. The first touch.

The day he held his hand out to me in that tavern, and then when I led him back to my place and gave myself freely and wholeheartedly to him. He claimed my first kiss. My first time.

Everything is his.

Moreover, I hated leaving. More than he'll ever understand, but as part of my promise, I returned that which I'd taken the first time. And maybe I didn't steal directly, Orion tried to claim it, but I held onto it and never let anyone wear it. Only my grandmother touched it for a short while; her health was on the line, and even that was hard for me to allow.

Jealousy is a powerful thing, and no one can touch what belongs to us.

I'll be with him soon.

The village is quiet tonight as I make a promise to the gods. This place is a hidden pocket near Bazra that is forgotten by time. It's tucked away between two cliffs and a dense forest, where no one asks questions or notices me.

Unless they're supposed to.

Magda's cousin, Elara, is one of those sharp-eyed people who miss nothing. She keeps tabs on me without ever making it obvious and has taken me under her wing, teaching me harmless spells and how to use herbs, when she isn't attending her shop.

She also explains passages in her cousin's book that at first glance make no sense, but with time, I've gotten better at reading between the lines. Like now, as the bell tolls on the shop door alerting her of my entrance, I pick up a bushel of lavender, some mugwort, and a few pieces of clear quartz before plopping myself next to her behind the counter.

"Just tell me if I am right," I say, opening to the page I'm reading and laying my spoils in front of it. "These three can help me sleep more deeply, calm my mind, and maybe even guide me into a more vivid, meaningful dream?"

"Correct."

"You don't sound impressed." Not a question, and she shrugs. "Fine. Hit me with it."

"That's child's play, and you know it. You're not a witch, but your abilities and intuition are sharp; don't deny it. Lean into it."

"Are you going to wax a poetic soliloquy on traditional herbs and their underrated usage in modern magic?" That earned me a flick to the forehead, but she was laughing, so I call it a win. Then her amusement slips, and I know this face. Serious. Worried. "You have news from Morvane?"

She nods, eyes assessing me. "Claims are circulating that Lord Severus has been...*impatient* lately. Annoyed by a certain visitor requesting his help in finding a family member."

"My grandfather?"

"Yes. He's been making the rounds a lot more frequently than usual." Elara hums, shaking her head. "Many in town are comparing him to a caged wolf, of all things. He's also asking about you, showing pictures, but no one's seen you with the cloak on. You're invisible, and it's creating problems that go beyond bringing a wayward granddaughter home."

My stomach tightens. "He's getting desperate, but why? What is he planning?"

"I'd know if you'd allow me to do a reading on you. Just a five-card spread would help here." The deadpan look that follows makes me want to flick *her.*

"Maybe next week?"

"Are you asking or telling?"

"Not sure, but I'm not ready to know how this plays out."

"It'd be a huge help, Neri." Whenever she calls me that, I'm reminded of Naia. We grew up together, went to school together, and shared so many milestones. From gaining our sharp little fangs, to one day waking up with breasts and having to have *the talk* with my grandmother, Naia was a constant at the palace, always spending more time with us than her family, and eventually she just moved in.

I treated her like a sister. Love her like family.

Yet she betrayed me, but how deep does that betrayal run?

"...besides, according to people who work in the old manor, your grandmother isn't doing well." That snaps me back to the present, a lump forming in my throat, but I remain quiet. Let her talk. "There are whispers about the stone, the one the women in your family gift to their mates, and the lack of one around King Atlas's neck. Not on his son-in-law's. Not on yours when you lived there."

"Why do I feel like this is about to get worse?"

"Because it is." Elara gives me an apologetic look, one laced with pity. "Nerissa, your grandfather is telling anyone who will listen that you stole it. That you hurt your grandmother out of hatred."

For the rest of the day, those eight words repeat in my head like a never-ending mixtape.

That you hurt your grandmother out of hatred.

It follows me to the coffee shop, the apartment I'm sharing with Elara, and then on my walk later that night. The moon's silver light casts long shadows along the wet sand while salt tangs the air. It's soothing and familiar, like a warm blanket you enjoy on cold days, and I keep close to the shoreline so the water can lap on my bare feet.

I try to reconcile the man I knew with who he is showing himself to be.

I try to test my reach beyond this beach, to pick up any lingering messages carried back to me by someone I love. Tonight, there is nothing but silence, until…

A scream rends the air.

It tears through the quiet, and my pulse leaps a second before I take off running. Feet pounding, I sprint toward the sound, sand slipping beneath my steps and I almost fall. It takes a second I don't have to lose to right myself, but I do, heart hammering against my ribs.

"Elara!" I yell out the closer to her shop I get, rounding the corner, and the world tilts into chaos. My friend, the woman who gave me refuge, is on her knees with a knife at her throat. Shadows move too fast for me to make sense of what I'm seeing—but I know.

Metallic. Old. Patchouli.

Vampires, elegant and cruel, terrorize villagers. They're breaking windows, smashing doors, and yanking innocent witches into the town's plaza. Some are pushed to their knees; others are herded to a cart, and I'm frozen in place until something strikes the back of my head.

Pain explodes and darkness claims me.

I DON'T KNOW how long I've been out, but I wake up in an opulent room so polished it hurts my eyes. Vintage florals, blood-red silks and velvet—gold picture frames and lighting fixtures with added gold filigree on everything. Multiples of them in every square inch of this space. Then there are the paintings: gardens, a wildflower field, and a countryside with more flowers. Lots of flowers.

Everything has flowers.

It all reminds me of something Magda loved to set on her coffee table: a mixture of dried petals, herbs, and sometimes fruits that didn't really smell like anything and always looked suspicious.

That's what this reminds me of. Too extra and untrustworthy.

A throat clears, and my head snaps toward the doorway, finding a man dressed in a uniform standing there. He's human. Of that I am sure, just like the pinched face and cold eyes make him someone I do not want to deal with.

"Come with me," he says, voice clipped, and my assessment was current. Uptight and rude.

"Where?" Not that he hears the question; the man's exited and is already down the hall when I rush after him. The place is cold, overly decorated, yet smooth beneath my feet. I'm led to what appears to be a dining hall, and all heads turn in my direction, some assessing me with interest while others look bored, the latter of which turn away and back to being fed on.

Vampires lounge like aristocrats throughout the room, their naked donors displayed like trophies. A copper tang perfumes the air.

And at the center of it all is Lord Severus. I know it's him because of the way the entire room surrounds him. He sits at a dais, chair high-backed and in a bloody red, with my grandfather standing mere feet from him, staring right at me. He's also in human clothes, a dark blue suit that isn't fitting him right, especially in the shoulder area.

"My child. I've missed you," Grandfather says. After being given a subtle nod, he approaches me as my eyes survey the room, looking for a possible exit, but that search ends when pain blooms across my face. What I thought was him coming to give me a fake hug is a literal slap in the face with enough force that I feel blood on my bottom lip.

I lick it, and multiple hisses come from the room, blood red eyes staring.

"This is unlike you, Nerissa. This is the act of an ungrateful, selfish girl." King Atlas is looking greyish, his cold eyes murderous, especially when he doesn't see the necklace around my neck. "While your grandmother suffers, you hide here, keeping the only thing that can save her."

"Or yourself?" That response earns me another slap, harder this time, and I stagger back but don't fall. My fists clench at my sides. Rage and fear surge within me. "If anyone has been the problem here, it's—"

"Enough." One word, and the room freezes as Lord Severus stands, pushing the woman on his lap to the floor, and walks over to me. In his hand, there's a white handkerchief, and without asking, he brings it to my lips. He dabs at the cut, his pointer finger skimming across a time or two. A drop of blood smears across it and he stares at it for a moment before licking it slowly, savoring it with a groan. "Simply delicious, Nerissa. You truly are a beauty."

"I apologize for all the trouble my granddaughter has caused, old friend. I'll be taking her home now and—"

"If you lay a finger on her again, I will forget our treaty and collect my debt."

"Understood. I acted out of fear and concern."

"Well, see you don't make that mistake again, Atlas. Don't tempt fate twice."

"Of course. Again, my apologies."

Through their exchange, I remain quiet. Don't say a word when I'm dragged out of the room by the arm, the cool air outside a much-needed reprieve from the cloying scents inside. Flowers, powders, and a bloody patchouli. It's like my mind is shutting down after the display inside the room. Between the slaps and being defended by a murdering vampire, I'm not that far from hysterics.

I'm also worried about Elara. Where is she? Did they hurt her?

Not that I'm able to think about it for long, as I'm knocked out again. This time, though, they drug me with Gods knows what, and I pass out, but not before I catch my grandfather speaking to someone.

"...we're not asking you to be a mistress forever, Naia. Just until after she gets pregnant and gives birth. After, we'll do what I should've done with her grandmother and lock her up."

"I don't want to hurt her, King Atlas. I just want my mate."

"And you'll have me, baby. Just help me impregnate the little brat first."

NERISSA

Twenty Two

The days blur. Or maybe it's been a week.

I've stopped counting altogether.

Time stretches in the silence of my newly gilded cage like a ribbon pulled too tight, each hour a weight pressing against my ribs. Thirty, forty…it doesn't matter when my cheek still aches where my grandfather's hands struck me, and Orion matched the act with a little vengeance of his own. Because the masks are off. No need to pretend to be a nice guy when the key to the kingdom is locked in a proverbial cage.

The bruises darken and fade with time, but it's the internal pain that's tearing me apart.

"I should've never run from him," I say to the open room. It's a beautiful cell, I'll give them that. With pearl accents, soft sea-silk bedding, and polished stone finishes, the room is bright and airy with a sophisticated feel. *They pamper with appearances and neglect everything else.* To the right, there's a small eating area where plates of old seaweed bread and kelp crackers await me, while to the left, there's the powder room. Not much else outside of the bed, and anything of entertainment value has been removed to help me reflect on my wrongdoings.

I move carefully from the bed to the chair, not wanting to be caught unaware by Orion, who's due for a visit. His daily lecture, and today, I'll welcome him with a stone to the head if he tries to kiss me again.

Yesterday, the general cornered me in the powder room while I brushed my hair and earned himself a slap, then my ornate brush slammed against his temples. He didn't like it and slapped me, re-aggravating my bruises, which I'm sure made him happy. Because the male ego, I've learned, is a fragile thing, and one word can send it into a tailspin of despair.

Victim blaming. Aggressor excuses.

Exhaling roughly through my nose, I try to find my calm before the interrogations begin. My fingers curl around the rock hidden beneath my dress, the only weapon I have to protect myself, and I sharpened it myself against the polished-stone table.

Its legs have just enough damage to be visible only if you really look at it, and they won't.

General Orion glides into the room at exactly two in the after-noon, dumping another plate of crackers before turning to stare me down. Sometimes he's polite. Others not so much. Today, I can tell it's going to be the latter. "Where's the stone, Nerissa?"

"I don't know what you're talking about," I answer, voice even. Face calm. My eyes meet his steadily, and I refuse to flinch. "You might want to be more specific."

Frustration ripples from him; he slams a hand on the table, sending all the uneaten bread and crackers to the floor. His sneer game is strong, too. "This is not a game, Princess. Where the fuck is the Cordis Lux? You're grandmother—"

"Correction—my grandfather. Get the facts straight." The silence that follows is thick, suffocating, and I let it settle around me like a familiar cloak. Unbothered. *Weeks of this, and I've stopped counting.*

Giving a single fuck. "Come back and see me when you have a better pitch, because right now, all you're doing is pissing me off, Orion. For once, be man enough to be honest and tell me what you need it for. What our *king* is truly after."

"With me, it would've hurt less. Have it your way." He leaves the room, and silence envelops me again. I think of Kai and my mistakes, how much happier I could've been if I'd spoken up and asked for help. The aches in my body are a constant reminder of the separation. Especially when I refuse to share dreams with him. In our dreams, he sees me as I am, and I don't want to worry him more than he already is.

Because I know what my expression will show.

Being without one's mate is uncommon and comes with physical consequences; I hurt.

My soul. My body. My heart.

How could Grandma live like this for so long?

Months apart, and to me, it feels like death, while she put up with it for over a century. She played the martyr, and for what? At the end of the day, she's still miserable without Ephraim. My mother would've understood, never held it against her mother, as she believed in the sanctity of fated unions.

Political alliances through marriage are a disgrace, unless both parties have been widowed.

He hasn't forgotten me.

Whispers I know to be true. I've heard things. The water carries secrets like sacred whispers; they travel far and always reach an audience, and with nothing else to do, I've made listening an art form. During the day, if I grab a chair and drag it toward the only small window in the room, one so small I could never swim through, and wait...

The gossip begins.

From the markets. From palace employees.

I hear it all, and my alpha's been busy looking for me. Destroying anything in his path, including the territories belonging to the vampires. Herds are being freed and the compounds burned to the ground, three in total so far.

I'm proud of him for that.

A thought that fades away when Naia appears. She looks fragile, worn down by her own battles, but sharp-eyed as ever. Still trying to read me like an open book, the problem is I'm no longer the same girl she knew from a couple of months ago.

"You...*Gods*, Neri. They took you," she whispers, and I'm not quite sure *who* she's talking about. Who is they? Because from where I'm sitting, she's part of that mess.

"Yup." Flat, my voice is lifeless and tired, but steady. "Here I am."

Naia swallows hard and her eyes grow glassy. "I'm sorry, Neri. So fucking sorry."

"And yet you helped them?" Accusatory? Yes. Am I going to apologize for it? Absolutely not.

"You don't understand...he...*fuck!*" She swallows hard, rubbing a hand down her tired face. "Orion did a partial claim to keep me by his side. I can't deny or resist him. It's literally impossible and he knows this, uses it against me, and I hate myself because I still love him." Naia's lips tremble. "He's my mate."

"How did you betray me?" My tail becomes legs before I realize what's happening and I'm pacing the room, back and forth, as I wait for the answer. "What exactly did you do?"

"You'll hate me."

I stare at her, taking in her exhaustion. The sheer helplessness on her face, and I want to smack, then shake her. Where's the sassy girl with grit and troublemaking tendencies that always ended up with us in stitches and our families shaking their heads?

Orion ruined her.

"Naia, as much as I love you, we will never be friends after this. You already lost me. At the very least, give me honesty."

"I told your grandfather and Orion about your home in Port

Avaria, your neighbors there, and the crush you have on *Alpha Daire.*"

She spits out his name with venom, and I move closer, my voice menacing. "Watch it, Naia. We both know you're the troublemaker, but I throw a better punch."

"How can you defend the man—"

"He's my mate."

"I see." Her face drops. Shoulders sagging. "Then I guess we have nothing else to discuss."

"No. There is something else." When we were kids, we used to have a game where the first one to laugh had to rush out and kiss a fish on the cheek. Random fish. Any fish. I won most of the time, and I apply the same rules now, staring deep into her eyes. This time, I'm just not making funny faces or noises. "Did you poison my father?"

"I didn't." But she looks away. "But I also didn't stop him."

"You and Orion will pay for every last thing you've done to me. Please leave."

"For what it's worth, Neri, it was never supposed to end this way. We were supposed to be best friends till the day we die, and because of that promise, I'm going to warn you now." Her voice drops, and her head tilts toward the door, checking for anyone listening. I already know no one's there. "In a few days, if they can't find the stone, they'll force you out of Marivelle and onto *his* territory. They'll leave you defenseless, naked, and tied to a rock if they have to, to draw out the alpha wolf. And once you're on board his ship, they'll attack, reclaim the stone, and drag you right back to the vampires for your wedding to Orion."

"Why are you telling me this?"

"Because I already lost you. I won't lose Orion, too."

"Your mate will die, Naia. By Kai's wolf, or my hand, but I will never submit."

"And I will return the favor." Her once friendly eyes are cold now, posture stiff. Neither of us willing to back down—the threat a promise. "Please don't make me kill you, because for him, I will."

"A sentiment we can both agree on." I stare at her retreating form as she leaves and mourn the friendship we had. Because I wasn't lying; we will never be the same again. The only thing that still holds meaning to me is exposing the truth and finding Kai again.

I'll endure for him, but I'll need a little nap to help center me.

Alpha
Kai

TWENTY THREE

The hunt has hollowed me.

Twelve months of chasing shadows, a full fucking year of tearing through ports that could've harbored her and setting fires to the one where herds were kept. We freed the humans and creatures found alive, sending them off to the eastern sea where colonies are setting up for the victims.

Am I a hero? No.

What I am is a man who's at his wits' end, but has faith the goddess will smile upon him.

My claws are stained with blood and brine. My wolf follows her call, and the last one brought me to a stretch of water between Isle San Tico and Isle De Lobos. I'm close to home, just a two-day sail either way.

The challenges are also a few days from now. Ships from all over the five seas are heading this way, all but the pack that betrayed their brethren and now serve the vampires. The northern pack has been seen making deliveries, transporting valuables across the sea, and I intercepted one right before it docked in Bazra, before changing ships to one of theirs.

The sea bled black with smoke as my cannons ripped their starboard open, splintering wood and bone alike as the mast snapped clean in half. Men screamed, and my wolves howled. The humans working with the northern pack did not know what to do as we attacked from all sides.

The injured ones couldn't do anything but lie there and pray for mercy, while the vampire's newly acquired pets tried to flee, but I was everywhere. Claws, blade, teeth—I plowed through anyone who raised a weapon against me and mine.

The deck was slick with blood, the charred flesh of the men who died and traitors who once again kneeled for me. Just not as part of my brethren, but as traitors.

My hand closed around a wolf dressed in the vampire guard's signature red, squeezing his neck tight. "Where's the scientist and his family? The rest of my wolves?"

"Back in Morvane," he wheezed, trying to fight my hold, but it was useless. My talon punctured skin; his blood dripped down my hand. "Please, I'm just following orders."

"Whose?"

"Our pack leader. He and the scientist made a deal with the—" I didn't need to hear any more. The confirmation of their treachery was all I needed, and I crushed his windpipe before tossing the guard's lifeless body overboard.

A few more followed the same fate.

Inside the hold, though, I found their treasure. Gaudy trash: gilded chairs and statues of gods they don't even believe in, crystal vases, and painting after painting after painting of different types of flowers. Décor from an era that no longer existed and was worthless to me; I dumped it overboard.

Let the ocean claim them. The only thing I kept were two chests of coins and a handful of scrolls marked with sigils I didn't recognize.

Gold had purpose. Knowledge had teeth.

The rest? Dead weight, and the two were left floating in open waters with a message for the Lord they serve. 'I wasn't done.'

"Where are you?" I ask out loud. It's beginning to drizzle, and I'm searching the area where we last met in our dreams. You brought me here with a promise, and I intend to collect.

"Alpha! To your right!" Maleth of all people yells out, and my head snaps in the direction he's pointing.

"Starboard," I bellow, spinning the wheel with so much force the spokes bite into my palms. My crew doesn't question or hesitate, Otto already rushing my way to take over while I help my men snap the sails. The deck tilts and a few barrels of rum break, but nothing matters more than reaching their luna.

Every single bit of gold could be reclaimed by these waters, and I still wouldn't give a fuck.

She's what matters. My Nerissa.

Reclining on a rock, she looks to be resting with nothing but a cloak covering her body. Her hair spills like ink into the tide, her skin glowing under the sunlight, but it's her stillness that has me jumping overboard and swimming toward her. I'm close, just a few more strokes, when those violet eyes open and set on me.

I'm set ablaze by her face. Having her this close.

She reaches for me, lips parting, and a song trembles free. Not the kind of melody that kills or glamours, but something sweet. It's raw yet soft, and it's unlike any other I've heard from her before.

I thought she'd sung for me before, but this resonates deep inside my chest, and a warmth unlike any I've ever experienced before covers me. From head to toe, I feel her. Like a caress. Like a fresh breath after being enclosed and lost for so long.

Relief crashes into me so hard, I almost pause, but that in and of itself would be a crime.

Against her. Against me.

"Little treasure." The pet name leaves me in a reverent whisper when I reach her. "Come to your male." A full-body shiver runs through her at the nickname—the command from her mate—before she throws her arms around my neck, pulling herself close, not an inch of space between us. A sob catches in her throat, her tears wet on my neck as tiny fingers grip my shirt tight. As if afraid I'll disappear. "I've got you, love."

"I knew you'd come." Her voice is low, a little scratchy, and I pull back just enough to get a good look at her face. While she hasn't lost weight, the heaviness in her heart shows in her violet eyes. "I had to do this, Kai. Please forgive me for the past, and what's coming."

"Nothing to forgive." My growl vibrates through her, and she finds this ticklish. It breaks a bit of the tension, especially when I do it again. When the laughs subside, I'm rewarded by her sagging against me, and I kiss the crown of her head. "You're mine, Nerissa. That's the only thing that matters."

"You know what they've made—"

"Enough. I understood perfectly, and all will be okay." I crush my mouth to hers, a quick yet harsh kiss. Her taste is mana on my tongue, and I take just enough to hold me over until I get us alone. Moreover, when she kisses me back just as desperately, I know this bond owns us both.

I trust her. Will stand by her.

When I finally tear away, I press my forehead to hers. "Never again, my siren. You vanish without telling me what's going on, or hide anything from me, and I will make the impossible possible."

"And what's that?"

"I will burn the seas until you're back pinned beneath me."

Her smile turns wobbly when her bottom lip trembles. "I'm dangerous, Kai."

"I'm worse."

The crew lowers the rope ladder, and I haul her with me, one hand on the rope and the other around my siren. I'm dripping and concerned, but whole for the first time in months. No one speaks as we make it back on deck, but they drop to their knees in a show of respect, and her little mouth drops open. It's adorable, and it's going to get very confusing in a few short hours.

In the meantime, I need to get her alone.

The pack members stay like that as we pass, Torren giving me a nod of understanding that I reciprocate with one of my own. No one will bother us. Not unless it's life or death, and I will kill anyone myself who does so without a good reason.

Across the deck, I carry her into my private quarters.

She's exhausted and shaking, the thin cloak doing absolutely nothing to protect her after days of shock. Nerissa lets me remove the fabric, but grips my hand to stop me before I place it on a chair. "Do you see the difference now?"

It takes me a moment to understand, but when I do, her beautiful scent dances around me like a fairy. It dances across my senses, the tethers of our half-formed bond stroking my cock.

"Motherfuck, Nerissa. How is this…?"

"A gift from my grandmother years ago. It cloaks my scent." Her smile is a bit cocky now, eyes playful. "Could probably mask a full ship if used as part of the sails. You know, hypothetically speaking."

"We'd have to test that theory someday, but for now…" I trail off, picking her up and tossing her onto my king-sized bed. She bounces a few times, tits juggling enticingly in all her naked splendor. A tiny doll, well over a foot shorter than me, she has curvy hips and enticing thighs. A flat stomach and high, perky tits with dusty rose nipples that complement her sun-kissed skin.

Long black hair, a cute button nose, and pouty lips.

Nerissa Del Mare is all that, an ethereal fucking beauty, but it's the violet eyes that hold me captive. They say so much when she's quiet, like now, when she beckons me closer with the crook of a finger.

The mattress dips and redistributes my weight after I take off my clothes, tossing them over the edge of the bed, and crawl over her. I'm covering her from head to toe, giving her my warmth as the wolf rubs under the surface of my skin. Not stretching, but scenting her through my skin so she carries a bit of us on her. She doesn't pull away when I do it, either. Instead, she patiently lets me drag my nose from one side of her neck to the other, leaving tiny trails of kisses in my wake.

I work my way down her body, collarbones, chest, stomach, and exhale roughly over her mound and back up again. Then her back and ass; not an inch of her hasn't been touched or kissed, and we purr with unadulterated pride when orange blossoms and coconut also carries notes of wood and leather. Even the tiniest bit of pineapple fills me with pure male satisfaction.

"Now, we can rest."

"Is that so?" Nerissa lies half on me and half on the bed, her leg across my cock. "Nothing else you want to do?"

"For tonight, yes." Tipping her face up to mine, I rub my thumb under her eyes. "You look exhausted."

"I've been worried. Haven't seen or spoken to my father or grandmother in a while." My hands begin to sweep up and down her soft back, the same way she traces the outline of a human skeleton on my torso. The point of her nails leaves a thin red line, as if she were playing Connect The Dots. I don't mind, revel in it, actually, because this is the most relaxed I've seen her. "Last time, Dad crossed paths with me in the western seas. His birth pod resides there. Much smaller than our royal grounds, but they're a fun and happy bunch."

"Did he give you any news on Lucienne? Was he going to be staying a while?"

"A vague update, and yes."

"Explain."

"So bossy." She admonishes, pinching my side, and I flash my teeth at her. Fangs and all. "And rude."

"Just that he'd be there a while, but was paying close attention. His older brother and his wife are helping him heal. And as for Grandma..." Nerissa bites me, not enough to break skin, but enough to leave a mark. "She's playing her role, and will remain by his side."

"What if he flips on her? Hurts her?"

"She's a strong mermaid and literally born a queen. She wasn't crowned through marriage, or for the sake of prosperity, but by her bloodline."

"So your saying never underestimate her?"

"Never underestimate a woman in general, Alpha."

"Noted."

We lay in silence after that, her body relaxed against mine while the ocean rocks us. It's lulling effect keeps us inside my room, warm and safe and oblivious to the outside world, until my look out sounds the alarm.

Then, it's chaos. Boots pounding and shouting, my door banged on while Torren yells through the wood, "Sirens!"

A chorus of chants, their song threading into the walls the closer they get. And unlike our last encounter, this time, it's all women.

My pack members are in danger. My ship is in danger.

Their songs grow louder, rousing my mate from sleep, and she hums a single note before rising to kiss my lips. Soft and private, the note is meant only for me, until the tip of a blade is pressed against my chest.

My knife. A clear quartz handle with a four-inch blade I keep close to my pillow every night.

Right against my heart, she whispers:

"The captain always goes down with the ship."

ALPHA KAI

TWENTY FOUR

"*The captain always goes down with the ship.*"

Threat. Promise. *Seduction.*

A low moan that settles on the tip of my throbbing cock while the pleasurable vibrations slide across every nerve ending like a filthy caress. Something she's aware of as her lithe legs wrap around my waist—her delicate fingers slipping into my hair and tugging hard—while her plump lips hum against my throat.

Her siren song. The cadence is sweet yet volatile—a provocative tease meant to heighten her delicious betrayal and my unwavering compliance. Because that's what this is: a play for power and revenge as she walks me out of the room, tip of the knife now pressed to my throat.

This is for control over what's been given and taken by her people more than once.

History repeats itself, and yet the players are a little smarter now.

I don't stop Nerissa as one of her hands leaves my hair and cold metal slips around my wrist a few seconds later, the loud click of the mechanical lock like a gunshot in the night. Firm. Sensual. Foreplay. Every muscle in my body contracts, the act painful as the animal—the beast within me—fights for control as she binds my other clawed hand to the large mast.

She planned this and somehow studied my ship; the proof is my now shackled arms.

The bindings are heavy and solid metal, not silver. Those are kept in the captain's desk.

These, though, are breakable. If I wanted to, I'd be out and mounting my siren, but I don't move. Instead, I let her play her game and set the trap, but *I'm* not the end target and we both know this.

Beautiful, cunning female. Mine.

Blood drips from my fingertips and onto the ship's deck. It marks the start of my hunt, and I snap my teeth playfully at her when the same dainty fingertips slide across each pointed tip of my right hand.

Back and forth. Gentle sweeps.

"You're such a good boy for me, Alpha. So sweet to his mate." Nerissa rolls her hips teasingly, almost lazily, while her sharp nails rake across my chest. No hurry. No self-awareness—acknowledgement of lighting my world on fire. Instead, the pointed yet delicate nails dig in deeper while the biting cold rain strengthens, stinging the newly made welts. A few tips break through my skin; I feel each drop and revel in the way she spreads my blood across her palm and my bare chest.

"And you're playing a dangerous game, my little treasure."

"Maybe I am..." she shrugs, a small tilt to her lips "...or maybe I'm too much for you, Alpha Daire."

My response? I buck my hips against her. The act causes Nerissa to let out an involuntary gasp, the knife slipping from her grip, but there's no fear there. No. The bond thrums between us, the high frequency demanding that I do just that...*claim* her.

Goosebumps rise across her skin, and her cheeks grow flushed. Moreover, it has nothing to do with the current humidity or the angry waves below us. The water crashes against the side of my ship, its power turning us, and there's no getting control of the helm when the heir to the merpeople's crown names me the *enemy*.

Taking in a deep breath, I hum as her scent envelops me. Owns me.

That delicious mix of orange blossoms and coconut with a hint of vanilla and something else—wilder and ancient—curls around my lungs. It hits me harder than the storm building around us ever could:

She's etched onto my skin like a tattoo. Rewires my blood to sing only for her.

I. Am. Hers.

What's more? She realizes just how mine she is, too.

There's no denying this. Us. We are, and it's as natural as the sun rising and setting or the tides crashing against the shore.

"Are you mad at me?" While Nerissa's tone is cocky, beneath the layer of challenge there's also a tinge of worry. Of caring. She's fighting against everything she grew up loyal to. Her family, the crown—her people. *Poor little mermaid mated to the one thing she's been taught to abhor above all else.*

"No. Not mad." I'm hard for the curvaceous nymph—fucking throbbing for another taste of the only cunt I'll ever worship—but she's dead set on setting my world on fire.

Or better yet, drowning it and then reviving us in a blaze of glory.

But then again, I wouldn't expect anything less from the siren who owns my beast and me.

Both man and animal belong to her now. Our fated one.

"Then what are you?"

"Indulgent." My one-word response has its desired response; her eyes narrow, and her lips form a pout. "Or were you expecting something else?"

"Careful, Wolf. Some might think you're still in charge here." Lightning cracks through the turbulent sky, striking the ship's bow then. The impact is sharp and jostling, cracking the wood where I embedded my claw marks above the carving of a wolf mid-shift, the day I laid claim to this vessel. The prior owner was an old pirate, a dishonorable shifter who challenged me for my alpha rank and lost more than his fangs that day.

Not the first time it happened. Won't be the last.

This ship was my prize.

My home for the last twelve months, while I hunted down my darling treasure.

I've fought like a beast. I've killed to protect it, too.

And now it'll all go down in a plume of smoke...

"What about now?" The lilt in her voice changes, pulling me back to those dangerous eyes. Her expression is gentler, a softness I enjoyed the night we met—before she stole from me and then ran. *Such a smart female. So perfect.* Nerissa's thighs loosen their tight grip around my waist, but she doesn't release me completely. No, she stays close enough to enjoy the vibrations coming from my chest in a low and soothing growl.

And it's in that closeness that I note the way luminescent scales in varying shades of purples and teal with touches of pink—different patterns—rise across her arms and ribs. They're beautiful, look so soft, but there's also a subtle thrumming coming from each.

Silent, yet they send a call that no one can hear, but then...

The mermaids below begin to sing again. Louder, their cadence meant to be sultry, and the tune is different this time. They're not going for subtle anymore. The melody intertwines with the howling wind, creating a hypnotizing soundtrack that my men fight against. Each note is meant to distract and control, lacing itself through the cracks in the wood and bone before coiling around every werewolf aboard like a velvet noose. Each note strikes an ingrained yearning every werewolf carries—the hunger for the softness of skin and the surrender of their fated bond.

A gift from the gods. Soulmates are to be treasured and honored.

Moreover, my pack doesn't believe in intimacy before finding your true mate.

We refuse to. We're loyal to our destiny.

Anything less would be a disgrace, no matter how long it takes to bond with your soulmate. And more than that, no wolf wants to be responsible for the pain that betrayal could cause their fated one.

We're territorial animals. We do not share.

The thought alone of another touching what is goddess-given and ours would lead to the death of a fellow shifter. There is no other way.

Yet my men aren't infallible, and the siren's song affects my crew.

One by one, they hit the deck, half-shifted—nails dragging splinters from the deck's wood as they struggle to anchor themselves. The song weaves, tightens, while a heavy crash comes from the bow of the ship. The carving and my claw marks are gone, lost in the turbulent waters below, while embers fly away in a plume of smoke.

"I'm going to make you pay for this, Nerissa. On your knees and then on all fours." Licking a fang, I taste her desire in the air surrounding us. There's no denying the scent of her wetness nor the hungry tug of the semi-formed bond between us. It demands we act. That we mark each other and fuck.

"They're here," she whispers low, mouth against my neck. You couldn't see or hear it from our position, the storm muffling any possible sound, and I give her a minute nod. "Remember, everything I do or say is a lie. Follow me when this is done."

"To the end of the earth, my siren. I love you."

"I love you, too, Alpha. Nothing will ever change that." Nerissa's smile is sweet, but then turns predatory as she unwraps her legs and slides down the front of my six-foot-five frame. The descent is slow, meticulous, and I snarl viciously when her wet cunt glides over my cock. "Now be good alpha and growl for me."

"I'm going to make you pay for this, Nerissa. You'll take it like a good girl and beg for more."

"Anything for you." A clicking sound comes from my mate, and the sirens come closer. They surround the ship, bodies positioned to attack anyone who tries to jump, and my men all fall into line. In our last shared dream, Nerissa had given me instructions for myself and my crew.

How to act. How to prepare for the compulsion to serve a siren.

Some of them have small pieces of cotton in their ears, blocking enough of the signal to lessen the effect. Their sounds are sweet and melodic—soaked in sin—while my female carries a slightly different tune meant to control me. Nerissa's song is private, a sensual call to her male, and my chest vibrates with an answering purr she can't ignore.

It's there in the rapid rise and fall of her chest. The dilation of her pupils and goosebumps on her soft, tanned skin.

"How much longer?" I mouth against her lips when she kisses me, while my pack members continue to fight. The ones without the cotton for help decided it was easier in their wolf form; they shook the noise off and grappled with their mouths to grab hold of the sail's rope. They bite and pull, dig their claws with a different purpose now, but nothing will save this ship.

I know it. They do too.

The mast snaps, the sails tumbling down and crashing a few feet from Nerissa and me.

"Get out. I'll find you later."

"But, Alpha—"

"Get them the fuck off the boat, Gamma. That's an order."

NERISSA

Twenty Five

"That's my beautiful treasure. Such a good little female worshipping her mate."

His praise excites me, more so because the show we're putting on only serves to anger Orion. I know he's watching, angry at my defiance and the sweet smile I give my wolf. A man who didn't doubt me or ask questions—Kai Daire only wants to make sure I'm safe.

This ship will not make it, and the only thing he asks for in return is that I remain loyal. That I come back to him. Two things he will never have to worry about as long as there is breath in my lungs and blood pumping through my veins.

I am his.

Taking him into the back of my throat, I slide my lips down fast and then drag them to the tip slowly, one hand skimming across his swollen knot, then lower to his balls. I squeeze and tug in a rhythmic sequence, giving him the bite of pain I've come to know he appreciates while the pleasure mounts as I worship on my knees.

From our position, no one can see me as he's facing away from the chaos, but they can hear.

Know that I am giving my mate his well-earned pleasure, and Orion can choke on that from wherever he hides.

Kai's grip on my hair tightens, and he forces me to look up at him. He pumps in lazily a few times, enjoying the control as water begins to lap at our feet. He's close, and I transition slowly, showing him the full effect of my skin turning from golden to a shimmering tail beneath the rising water as what's left of the mast groans. He does, too, as I use my tail—flick the fin back and forth—to keep me at just the right height to fuck his cock.

But it's the look in his gorgeous honey eyes that drives me to hungrily hiss out, "Mine."

"I'm yours, Nerissa. Take what you need."

"Never forget that, Alpha," I say, and this time, when I sucks him in, I don't stop until reaching his knot. There, I tighten my lips and tease the underside with the tip of my tongue...

"Gods, sweetheart. Perfect fucking mouth," Kai hisses out from between clenched teeth as the first rope of his spend lands on my tongue. And I hum at the taste, hollowing my cheeks and bobbing faster to milk every last drop.

I'm blushing as I do. The heat on my face spreads from the apple of my cheek down to the tops of my breasts, but then it all crashes into us. Sounds get louder. Yelling is desperate.

Gods, everything slams back into focus as we take full breaths.

The late-night sky is lit up by the storm, and rain begins to pelt hard just as the water reaches his chest. The weight of the broken mast is dragging him down, dark water surrounds us, and yet I'm not concerned.

Those shackles will not keep him down, but a flash of pain still crosses my features. More so when I sense General Orion behind me.

He tugs on my arm, but I yank myself away, turning in time to see my wolf break free.

And as planned, I swim past him and yank the stone from his neck. The wolf flashes behind his eyes, our bond trying to reassure me as the mermaids surround their fallen princess. It physically pains me to swim away from him, but I do. I want to extend my hand to him, tell him I will come back, but the formation grows tighter as he watches them take me away.

Yet there's no mistaking the voice that croons in my head as I'm hauled onto another ship a few miles away. *I'm coming for you, my sinful treasure. There's no escaping me.*

THEY HAUL me onto another ship, rough hands biting into my arms as if I were a thief caught mid-crime and not the heir to the Del Mare throne. The air here tastes different, a little colder, and I look around and take note of the late evening fog and humid temps. I know we are way outside of Mar de Sombras and slipping into the western territory.

A mistake that could turn out helpful to me.

My father's pod is from these waters, and they keep precise account of who enters and exits the territory. I clear my throat, and all eyes turn to me. There's so much judgment in them, reproach, as I'm paraded toward what I think are the captain's quarters.

Then again, it's not every day that a mermaid is dragged before vampires, fin still in place. Once outside of the water, we tend to shift, but I want them to see me as I am. Proud, unapologetic, and I will not bend to the will of over-inflated egos.

The few mermen on board are part of the guard, the females have already performed their duties and should be resting in Marivelle with a spread of cakes, jams, and sea grapes to soothe their throats.

I'm offered nothing but judgment with each step closer, my guard's chin raised high while others hiss behind my back.

Let them look. Let them choke on it.

The door is flung open as we approach, and it rattles against the wall. Inside, the scent of blood and powder is suffocating, as is that gods-awful décor this clan of vampires seems to enjoy. Not because flowers or crystals or gold accents can't be pretty, but because of the kind they choose. The obscene amount added into every nook and cranny makes each square inch feel suffocating.

My eyes land on my grandfather's first. He sits behind a carved table, spine regal, and eyes gleaming with command. Beside him, Naia keeps her head down, and the inability to so much as look at me speaks volumes.

To the left is Lord Severus in full regalia, as if we were heading to a royal ball and not the archaic fiasco my own kin have cooked up. He's as still as a statue, pale and draped in heavy fabric, a shadow draped in flesh, with his crimson gaze roaming from my tail to my neck and back down again.

Each time I swallow, he licks his lips.

My heart accelerates, and he looks to be counting the heartbeats for his ledger.

But it's my grandmother who steals my breath. Off to the side, bound in chains, she looks worn and fragile. Yet at the sight of me, relief softens her gaze. Relief and hope reflect at me, her nod barely perceptible, and I, too, breathe a little easier.

She's received my message before this happened, and my father is coming. Other sirens will join this fight. Not showing her too much attention, I square my shoulders and stare at the man I once looked at as a second father figure.

Unshaking. Unbreakable.

"Your Majesty," one of the guards who dragged me in says, his hand on my shoulders, trying to shove me low but I remain standing. I don't shift or kneel, much less give these people the show they are looking for.

"He should've never been our king." My words are met with a few gasps from those who are part of the army, while Orion moves in closer. He'd let them drag me; he didn't want to dirty his hands after my little performance.

Had I known what a delicious little submissive whore you are, I'd have broken this spirit years ago, Princess," he whispered right before we'd broken the surface. The others had swum away, but he lingered long enough to deliver his venom. *"You'll choke on my cock, cry tears of joy, and then thank me for using your filthy, mutt-loving mouth when I'm done."*

"Watch yourself, Nerissa. Don't make me hurt you." Orion's threat doesn't land well with everyone; the vampire hisses at him in warning.

"Do not hurt her, or the deal is off."

"Neri, please…" Naia starts, but that's as far as she gets when I narrow my eyes at her.

"You are no one to address me with such familiarity. Our friendship died when you betrayed me."

"I did it for love."

"No, you did it for your convenience. The desire to be more than what you are." My words land like barbs, precise and cutting. She flinches, silently begging me to drop it, but I'm past being the understanding, caring friend. "Had you come to me, I would've helped you—spoken to my family and found you a higher-ranking position within our palace. Because in your delusional mind, you're not his equal, when in reality, Orion isn't worthy of you."

"Enough!" My grandfather stands, slamming his grayish hand atop the table, and an antique porcelain tea cup tips over, shattering upon impact. The shards spread, the dark brown liquid inside ruining the rug beneath him. Big mistake, as Severus stands and stalks across the room, his hand gripping my grandfather's throat tight.

Atlas is lifted off the ground, his smaller body clawing at the old vampire's hands. "Your attitude bores me, Merman. I warned you to keep things civil, to not threaten her, and yet you disobeyed me twice. One more, and I'll execute you now and name her queen."

If he thinks I'll thank him, Severus is mistaken, and I turn my attention back to Orion.

"My crown. My blood," I spit out, voice carrying sharp across the room. "Never forget that, Orion. I'm not some nameless woman you can command at your will, nor will I ever drop to my knees for you. Your biggest mistake is confusing manners for submission... you're unworthy, egotistical, and blinded by a level of self-importance that astounds."

His jaw ticks, eyes leaving me to look at the vampire holding his king. "Quit while you're ahead."

I snort at that, turning to the woman I once called my best friend, instead. "What do you see in him, Naia? What kind of a mate hurts his beloved, only to turn around and use her again and again?"

That had to sting more than one person, especially with how Atlas murdered Severus's goddaughter for similar reasons.

"This is not why we're here," the vampire cuts in, his voice controlled. Low. "This is supposed to be a celebration between species, and my donor isn't happy. That makes me even less agreeable to what you've asked of me, Atlas. Fix this."

"What are you talking about?" I ask as renewed dread fills me. Especially as Severus, with his grip around my grandfather's neck, walks him over and presents him to me. On his knees, the mermaid king looks up at me. "What did you do?"

"You're to wed Orion tonight, under the new moon."

"No."

"You have no choice, Nerissa. It's this, or your grandmother dies." Six words, and they bring nothing but horror to me. Dread. I knew coming here they'd have plans to marry me and Orion, but not today. Certainly not when I have no idea just how close Kai is. "It's the only way to keep her breathing, and you by her side, my child." His gaze drops to the stone in my grip. I'd forgotten about it, my focus on keeping calm and stalling for as long as possible. "Don't think of it as bad, but rather a joyous occasion. We'll get the stench of wolf off you, perform the ceremony with the help of my wife, and then seal the bond with a bite. Nothing too hard, and think of it as an investment, versus squandering your legacy on that filth."

Orion steps in when I don't respond. My shock doesn't allow it, his hand wrapping around me before I can pull away. His grip is iron tight, and I grimace, especially when his nails dig into my side. "It must be done, Neri. I promise to cherish this gift and remain faithful."

A pain-filled sound comes from Naia, hurt laced with anger, but she doesn't say a word.

Pain lances when his unoccupied hand covers mine and the stone. It burns, but not from heat—the outright refusal of a mating, and then nothing. It grows arctic cold, and for a second, I wonder if it'd shatter on its own rather than take what is not freely given?

Orion snarls and tries again, pressing his forehead against mine like a force can rewrite fate, but the stone remains still. "What did you do to it?"

"Nothing. Just standing here."

"Or maybe you forgot a simple rule about magic." It's my grandmother's voice that cuts through. "You're trying to force her, and magic, much like love, needs to be coaxed. Not taken, but freely given."

Dusting himself off, her husband stands to his full height and narrows his eyes. The vampire has moved to stand against the back wall, almost blending in, while Orion paces. Mutters to himself.

"Tell me, Lucienne. What did I do wrong?"

"You perform the wedding first. A crimson union."

ALPHA KAI

TWENTY SIX

I break through the surface, feeling the contradicting cool breeze and the heavy scent of smoke infiltrate my senses. It's overwhelming; thick and choking. Even with most of the ship swallowed by the sea, the smell clings to the area as I float in my human form.

My wolf is resting. Amused. Content. Relaxing. He's all but taking a nap while the low, rhythmic pull of oars carries over the waves. Longboats move closer, my pack members staring as they pull up beside me.

They're fighting back grins.

"Our Alpha rises from the deep," Torren calls out, his tone laced with amusement. "Thought our luna might've drowned you."

A chorus of chuckles rings out. Obnoxious and contagious; I flip them off. This causes them to laugh harder, the vessel rocking now, and I'm fighting back my own grin as I pull myself up. It's made worse when my movements almost tip us over, and I'm half tempted to push my gamma and his brother overboard as I plant my bare feet on the slick wood.

"I'm kind of proud of her," Otto interjects, lip curling at the corner. "She destroyed our alpha's ship, tricked the mermaids, and pissed off their bitch of a general in the process. Fucking brilliant."

"I second that."

"Me too," a chorus calls out in unison, and my beast goes from sleepy to ruffled. He growls low in my chest—the warning clear. *Mine.*

"Keep talking, and I'll make you swim behind my ship."

"What ship?" Maleth asks, brows furrowed. I point behind us. Our pack's biggest ship looms on the horizon, flanked by twenty or so other ships.

They slice through the dark waters, black sails straining against the wind—a declaration of war. The Five Seas have answered. Wolves from every pack, from every corner of the waters I rule, sail beneath banners that snap like whips in the night.

This year's challenge will be different, I'd sent word out with the change in the rules. Blood will not be spilled for dominance or tradition.

This is for honor. For loyalty. To protect our people.

For our luna.

I'm coming for you, love.

Shots ring out, followed by the thunder of small cannons. The sky ignites, each boom a pulse through my chest. The hunt has begun.

Maleth, who'd been standing to my left, leans closer. His voice low. "Once you find Severus, and he'll be on that boat, I'm claiming my kill. Following."

I tilt my head. "Following?"

"He'll run."

"How do you know that?"

Maleth's silver eyes sharpen, his stare meaningful. Respectfully, he meets my eyes, needing me to understand *why*. His truth.

"Because my father is a coward, Alpha. He's not a fighter, but an opportunist. And once that *opportunity* slips from his cold, dead fingers, he'll save his ass."

"He doesn't get away, Maleth."

Placing his hand over his chest, he nods his head. "You have my word. He will die."

NERISSA

Twenty Seven

I stare at myself in the mirror, fog rolling in from the sea like a living thing, thick and curling around the ship. It's hard to see anything past the plume, and I pray that just beyond the physical manifestation of my fear is my wolf. That his boats are nearby, and my family didn't turn their back on me when I needed them the most.

My chest rises and falls with each pull of the damn electric air. It's slipped in from the open window, humming as I put the final touches on my costume. Grandma Lucienne watches me, nervously wringing her free hands as I slip into the wedding attire for my people. How, without meaning to, I make a spectacle of what we value as traditions.

The bra, a delicate opal coral bead, catches the muted lights as I turn in the mirror. Each bead is chosen with care, contouring over the slopes of my breasts and covering, framing each nipple in a way that isn't obvious but if you look hard enough, you see the bare tip.

It's meant to highlight what now belongs to your mate. A tribute for him to uncover and covet, making it impossible to last past the ceremony, and you retire early to the marital suite. In a true ceremony, I'd be in my tail until the bite, and then everything is fair game. Today, though, I'm in a thin and billowy skirt, the white material shifting with each minute movement, with a slit that reaches my hip.

No underwear. Nothing in my future husband's way, and I shiver in disgust at the thought of being tied for life to Orion. Every step must be careful, measured, and with self-awareness.

I refuse to flash anyone.

Grandmother Lucienne steps in beside me, her delicate hand on my shoulder, pushing the long strands out of the way. "Nerissa, your father and the family pod—everyone is here. Beyond the fog, twenty pirate ships are ready to strike, with Magda and Elara holding the cloaking illusion up. Smart move on giving Kai the robe."

A breath of relief escapes me, and I bite back tears. "He came?"

"I'm right here." He walks out from behind a floor-to-ceiling velvet drapes. I'm shocked it could conceal his frame, but the position of a high-backed chair in front of it masks his size. That, and an armoire directly beside it in the same finish as the chair. Dark wood, thick fabric, and so many little trinkets that the eye is too busy taking everything in to play *find the alpha.*

"When did you…?"

"Doesn't matter." Within seconds, I'm being lifted off the ground and kissed, my earlier red lipstick wiped off with the onslaught. It's deep and lingering, and I'd gladly give up my last breath to never stop feeling those lips on mine. Footsteps come closer, the wood creaking, and he pulls back long enough to look me up and down. Give my nipple and the beads a quick tug. "You look gorgeous, smell amazing, and taste even better. I want to claim you wearing this, little treasure. Don't let Orion touch a single bead."

The possessiveness in his tone has my thighs clenching, but the look in his eyes makes me whine, a sound my grandmother raises an eyebrow to. "Don't judge."

"Not at all." From a pocket in her dress, she pulls out a small switch blade with a clear quartz handle and a ribbon of sea-silk. *I thought I'd lost it. How did she find it?* She places both in my hand, the reason very clear, and I secure it to my thigh in a way that it appears part of the attire. My heart tightens, throat dry in gratitude. *Thank you*, I mouth, but she shakes her head, placing a small kiss on my cheek. "All I want is your happiness, my child."

"And I yours. It's never too late to claim Eph—"

"Quiet. Someone's at the door." A second later, someone tries to turn the handle but finds it locked. That gives Kai time to slip into place again, my grandmother unlocking the door before taking a seat in front of the curtain. "Come in."

I catch his scent before I see him. But there he is in the reflection of the mirror.

Clean, polished, and regal for a disgraced king. In his hands is a small stack of papers with a pen, but for a few seconds, he doesn't meet my eyes. Instead, he eyes the stone. Always the stone, and I'm starting to believe it's a case of wanting what isn't yours.

He had the crown. He got to marry the true heir and use her connections,

Riches. Respect. Even love for a while, but it was never enough for him.

"I know it may seem like I don't love you, Nerissa," he says softly, too softly as he fixes his suit jacket. All red, too. "But this must be done. Not just for me, but for our future. The kingdom deserves the kind of leader who will put us first, not forget who the enemy is."

"You mean the story you made up?" My expression is deadpan, and I'm grateful he's not paying attention as I clean up the mess from my lipstick. "That enemy?"

"Just do the right thing, Nerissa. Make this easy on everyone and sign this."

The one he speaks of? A four-page contract listing my duties as the new mermaid queen and caretaker of the needy. I bite back my retort on the ridiculous title and continue to read, growing angrier by the second.

- Twice a month, blood donation to Lord Severus only. No sexual contact unless requested and your husband allows. Compensation benefits both parties.
- Sole caregiver for all children born from the union—and if Orion chooses to have a child with his mate, Naia, I will care for those, too.
- Confinement in a high tower with Lucienne. Presence solely requested for official ceremonies. Queen in title only, duties handled by the new royal assistant, Naia St. Cruz
- Naia and Orion will share a marital bed, as she's his fated mate. I will perform my sexual duties in a separate chamber, prepared for the entertainment of King Orion.
- Duties will begin as soon as I marry.

"You find this garbage fair?" I murmur, voice cutting as the raging, simmering within threatens to overtake me. The blood in my veins throbs, my muscles coiling tight before I strike. I want to. To grab the knife from my thigh and unleash this pent-up hate that is robbing me of breath as I watch the man I thought so highly of try to barter my life away for his benefit.

I will not bow. I will not submit.

Grandfather leans in, his voice a cheap honey over rusted steel. "Don't be difficult. Sign this, and maybe I can talk Orion into sharing you with the wolf. An agreement can be made, a Monday through—"

"No." I'm shaking my head so hard that an earring falls. "I will not be sold as a breeder whore who part-times as a blood escort while taking care of other people's babies like a glorified nanny. How could you even ask me to sign something so demeaning? To give up my life and freedoms in exchange for servitude?"

"Nerissa, I will not be—"

"What part did you not understand, Atlas?" My grandmother stands, walking over to us in a red dress that isn't her normal style. She prefers soft tones, not that I think she had much of a choice in this, like me. This entire *wedding* is being put together by the vampires. Their taste. *Is that what she meant by crimson union?* "Let the kids marry first. The rest can be handled after."

That surprises him. Me too. But he agrees, especially when Severus walks in a minute later, dressed in red from head to toe, and offers me his arm. "Your groom is waiting, little one."

It's hard, but I fight back the urge to cringe at the pet name. Just no.

Kai is the only man I will ever accept any term of endearment from.

Turning around, I pretend to touch up my lipstick a final time, fluff my soft, dark waves…

I'm stopped by the words etched into the bottom right-hand corner of the mirror. I didn't see it until now, the light letters hidden by vain distractions, as my great-grandfather used to say, but the message hits home—today more than ever:

What your heart desires is
never truly lost.

You fight for it. You take it.

They escort me to the top deck, my grandmother sending me a wink no one catches.

There's red and gold everywhere. Even the sails are crimson, catching the moonlight through breaks in the fog. An archway is near the helm, like a raised dais where those here to witness will watch a woman demean herself in the name of tradition and sexism—the sale of her self-worth in the name of egotistical pride.

This will be a crimson union; I will make sure of it.

The small dagger feels cool against my skin as we pause long enough that all heads turn in my direction. The mermen have changed into human skin and stand with the vampires, appraising the future queen as if she were an object and not someone's little treasure.

Then I find Naia. On her knees, Orion has his hand on her head, patting it. She's in tears, while he smiles at those in attendance. Exchanges a few words with the man officiating the ceremony.

"This is unbelievable," I mutter under my breath, but Severus catches it. His hand pats mine in the crook of his elbow. Planning to give me away as if we were family.

"Looks exquisite, doesn't it?"

"Sure does."

"We wanted the best for you, Nerissa. To make this as pleasant as possible." Somehow, I think that's more to do with him than the other two. They'd be happy to force me to sign and then bite me so hard, I'm in pain for days after. I don't say any of this, of course. Instead, I force a small smile onto my face that could be confused with gratitude. "Now, let's get you down the aisle."

From somewhere, an organ starts to play, and we take the first step.

It feels like stepping into a trap. Orion's grin turns cocky, as if he won. My grandfather beams with pride, his arms around my grandmother, whose eyes are on something in the distance. Reflective and small. The vampire walking beside me tilts his head, eyebrows furrowing a second too late.

Guards collapse under the first strike.

Wolves hidden by the fog leap onto the ship. They surround the deck from both sides, scaling the sides in human form before transforming into beasts, and large paws hit the wood. Some of the older pieces crack under the weight, but that only spurs these killers into taking down anybody deemed an enemy with them. A few vampires are the first victims, falling on the large wooden pieces sticking up in the air.

Their cries are short-lived, while the panicked song of sirens rends the air.

They're trying to call out to anyone nearby for reinforcements, but that's their second mistake. My father is the first one on the ship, followed closely by my uncles and cousins—every member of the Azure pod is here, and they are brutal. Some have swords, others use spears, driving the blades in deep without a single ounce of remorse.

In the chaos and screaming, Orion reaches me as Lord Severus runs inside. I lose sight of him the same way the merman general has forgotten his mate on the dais; she screams and cries, but those crazed eyes are on me. "Did you call them here?" I don't answer him. Instead, I take two steps back. "Answer me, you bitch."

We follow this game until I'm back by the entrance to the captain's quarters, and his hand shoots out to slap me. It never makes contact as a large clawed hand grips and catches his hand, snapping the bone in two before reaching back and patting my thigh.

Orion screams, stumbling back in pain while Kai, in his half-shift form, removes the blade from its makeshift holster. "Do you want the honors, little treasure?" he asks, the garbled voice deep and power-ful; it runs through me, and I shiver in both lust and excitement. One, because he came for me, and two, because it's a true honor when a predator offers you his kill. "Or do you want me to handle it?"

It. Not a man. Not worthy of having a name.

"Can I have first strike?"

"You can have anything you want." Alpha Daire lunges after the general, who's trying to slink away toward the banister. He almost makes it, too, but is then dragged back for me. Orion's kicked in the back of the knee and made to kneel, looking at me as I grip the dagger and drive it straight into his eye, twisting it. The sound it makes is wet, then a pop, and drops him with a sickening thud. Did I kill him? Possibly, but I'm not given the chance as my mate lifts me, wraps an arm under my bottom, and stomps a foot through his chest on his way to the other side of the ship.

"I'll kill her. Stand back," a voice I'm all too familiar with booms, and every merman stalks forward, closing in on my grandfather when a loud, angry growl fills the night. Another black wolf jumps onto the ship; its animal has a few streaks of grey along its ears, and its eyes are set on my grandmother.

Her eyes become glassy, a few tears falling at the sight of him, and the stone I'd carried around my neck comes alive. Blue and bright, and it vibrates as my mate nuzzles the side of my head.

"Ephraim, I'm—" She's cut off by a low chuffing sound, almost a chuckle or maybe a chide, but Lucienne submits to the sound. The wolf, like my mate, can stand on his two hind legs and turn into something that's the perfect balance between man and wolf. His features come forward, a handsome man with a few scars from age, but just as handsome as my mate. *I'm a very lucky siren.*

"Come to me, Lucienne. It's been too long." Her body moves, tries to shove Atlas away, but the latter only presses the knife deeper. My grandfather mumbles something, curses ever marrying her, but it's the first drop of blood that signs his death warrant. Ephraim's hand shoots out and yanks my grandmother into his arms, kisses her forehead, and then places her behind him.

It all happens so fast after that. Blood everywhere. Guttural cries.

He tears into him with claws and teeth, ripping chunks of flesh from his body, and I have to look away from the gruesome scene. I hear it, though. The anger. The utter brutality, until there's nothing left but a mangled heap that soon after hits the water.

I should feel sad, but I'm not. I should demand they stop, but this is a necessary evil.

One by one, every merman, vampire, and siren left is made to kneel as wolves make quick work of the enemy. All but the vampire lord, who seems to have disappeared the moment the attack began. They've searched the boat, but he's nowhere to be found. The same goes for Maleth...

My father and our family collect any flammable item on this ship they can find, while Magda and Elara step into view, lighting the pyre. They smile at me in my mate's arms, the affection genuine in their eyes, until I feel something sharp slice into my arm.

Not deep, but it burns, and Naia is given no mercy as she screams her hate. "You don't deserve to be happy, Neri. You took everything from me, like the selfish—" Kai's hand punches through her chest, tearing out her heart. Quick. Painless. A mercy kill for what an alpha wolf is capable of for his mate, and I'm thankful. A piece of me will always care for her, but she chose this path.

To take and take as long as it served her. No care for anyone but her, and I can't blame it all on the mate bond. They were brainwashed into thinking everything they did was justified as good for the kingdom.

"She can follow him into the afterlife," Kai spits out, grabbing my arm gently and turning it to see the cut. It's small, red, but not really bleeding. "Does it hurt?"

"I'm more than fine, handsome." He likes that, a slight pink crossing his cheeks, and I fall at that moment all over again. The past year has taught me a lot. Patience, trust—to enjoy the small moment because at the end of the day, those matter the most. This is one of those. "Let's go home."

"Only if you do me the honor of accepting my bite one week from today in front of our sirens and wolves."

"It's a date, Alpha Daire." With both hands, I cup his cheeks and lay my forehead on his. Share my aura, breathe in his every exhale. "Now, kiss me. I've missed you."

ALPHA
KAI

TWENTY EIGHT

The beach burns with firelight, the sea alive with song.

Werewolves stand shoulder to shoulder with sirens, voices carrying into the night as the gods themselves have come to watch. It's a knowing, this feeling of peace and rightness that fills every creature witnessing our union.

From her grandmother standing beside my grandfather, their fingers intertwined and smiles bright, to her father—my parents—and everyone who's stood next to us. Those who fought to break the curse of greed and hate. This celebration is for all of them, to the end of a tradition that will no longer be practiced, my grandfather will keep the stone—we don't want it.

But mostly, this is for *her*. Our glue. My Nerissa.

Everything starts and ends with her.

My female. My mate.

Nerissa walks barefoot toward me, a gauzy white skirt shimmering around the scales visible beneath her skin. Purples and blues with touches of pink, beautiful colors that contrast against the light, and she's never looked more beautiful. Ethereal.

My chest strains with the need to meet her halfway, to throw her over my shoulder and stalk into the woods to claim what's mine— but this is a sacred moment I'll cherish for the rest of my life.

Our vows. Our love.

Because I do love this woman. With everything I am and will be.

The high siren's voice rises above the waves. "Before the gods of the sea and earth, wolf and mermaid, you stand to pledge your lives to each other. To walk this life together, never forsake the other, and come together as one when in crisis or hurt. She is yours. You are hers."

"I do."

"I do, too," Nerissa whispers, her bottom lip trembling.

"Turn to look at each other and speak your vows."

A sudden lump catches in my throat, but the words come out rough and true. "Nerissa Del Mare, my storm, my little treasure. I vow to protect, love, and cherish you for the rest of my days, until the goddess calls me home. I will fight at your side, but never against you. I will shoulder the storms when they get too heavy and you need a break, the same way you ease my tempest when the world tests my limits." Tears fall from her eyes, and I wipe each one slowly. With reverence. "I love you, Nerissa. Today and all my tomorrows."

"Kai, that was unfair." Around us, our families laugh, while those beautiful violet orbs shine. "My wolf. My anchor. My home. I vow to love you without conditions, to walk every path with you, and to be your compass so you always find your way home. In this life and every one that follows, I ask the gods to bless me with you as my partner. As the love of my life."

"The gods bear witness to this beautiful bond and bless it with an eternity together." My pack howls at that while her sirens sing, the song a tune of celebration and life. Happiness fills the night. My heart is at peace, but it all fades away when I crush my mouth to hers. She tastes like sin, like everything right in the world and that I fought to be worthy of.

"Mine," I growl against her lips. The need to finally mark her can no longer be ignored, and to the sounds of cheers, my wolf comes forward but doesn't take over. This is a special moment for the two of us, and when she breathes out a, *"Yours,"* I'm done for.

Scooping her up with one arm, I toss her over my shoulder and walk us into the woods. Roars of approval follow, both pack and pod happy, their fists beating against their chests.

Nerissa laughs at that, but she doesn't tell me to stop. She knows where I'm taking her.

The woods welcome us, shadow and moonlight wrapping us in privacy, and I set her down only when I can't stand another minute without her bare for me, her skin pliant under my touch.

"I love you, Nerissa, and I thank the gods above for crossing our paths." Drawing her scent deeply into my lungs, I close my eyes for a moment and savor her decadent scent. I taste her in the air around us, this unique blend of salty and sweet that's currently lashing my flesh as if her siren essence were a whip.

Marking me. Owning me.

"And I don't just love you, my alpha...I belong to you. With every breath, every act—my soul has always been yours."

"Goddess help me," I grunt as my fangs drop, cutting my bottom lip. It's a small wound, no more than a few drops of blood slipping, but her subtle gasps only serve to call the beast forward a little more. My black-tipped claws break through, and fur rises across my skin as all my senses settle on her.

My siren. My life.

"Come to me." My voice is gravelly with hunger, the deep timbre little more than a growl from deep within my chest. A sound that affects her as her scent deepens with a sharper note, one that pulls drops of pre-come from my engorged tip. Her essence strokes me while the precious little mermaid watches me as if I were a sacred, cursed wonder.

My cock gives a harsh jerk beneath the confines of my trousers, and I rip them off, cursing anything that keeps me from her. Skin to skin. Moreover, her entire body trembles at the sight.

Thighs are squeezing tightly. Nipples pebbled into high peaks; the beads of her bra are a light yellow in honor of my wolf's golden eyes. And yet, that's not what I'm drawn to.

I'm captivated by shimmering scales beneath her human flesh. Iridescence in shades of blue, pink, and that same unique purple that matches her eye color. *Fucking beautiful.*

"Come to me, little treasure. Let me mark that pretty little neck, then worship you like the good girl you are."

"Like this?" She drops her skirt to the ground, stepping away from it before moving the triangles of her ceremonial bra aside, making it look like a necklace now. Ornament for the skin I'll break, then heal with my tongue. She steps closer and lifts her hair off her neck, then lets the strands fall slowly in a tease before giving this predator her back.

I'm behind her in an instant, my arm around her midsection and flipping her around so we are face to face. I position her tight, wet heat above my cock. The head kisses her opening, testing her slickness before I lower her fully to me. Her feet are off the ground, her slick hole fighting to fit my knot, as I bring my lips to her ear.

"Do you accept my bite and knot, Nerissa Del Mare, as a sign of my ownership and devotion to you? Both are solely yours, as I forsake a life where you aren't mine, as I am yours."

"Yes. Please."

"I accept you, too, love. Mark your wolf." Her face turns toward me at the same time I bite down, breaking the skin where shoulder and neck meet, and her blood coats my tongue. It's heavenly, sweet, and salty—a part of my DNA now.

"*Oh, fuck,*" she moans, her teeth digging in deeper to my jaw, and a full-body shiver runs through her. The bond fully snaps into place, and it's a wondrous thing to feel what she does, to hear the filthy thoughts running through her head, and the last one has me bracing my feet on the solid earth below.

Knot me, Alpha.

My hips punch up, and at the same time, she uses my shoulders for leverage, working a quarter of my knot into her small hole.

"Goddess, baby. That…I need to—"

"Rut me, Kai. Claim me." She's off my cock and on all fours before her next inhale. A squeal falls from those perfect lips, and the sound is like a stroke down my shaft. I need more of that sound. To hear it for the rest of my life. My claws dig into the ground, fangs skimming up the back of my little treasure's neck as I cover her body with mine. *Fuck, she's perfect.*

My solace. My home.

On all fours and with her holes exposed to nature—given to me as a gift—I rub the head of my cock over each. From her ass to cunt, I spread her slick a few times, pulling a delicious whine from those plump lips. Then again. I do this three more times and slam in deep.

This isn't sweet or soft. I fuck my queen like a beast. My claws dig into the ground on either side of her, tearing through the earth while my hips pick up the pace. There's no reprieve or pause, and when she comes with a long, drawn-out moan, I kiss the back of her head and thrust forward a final time.

"Son of a bitch." My knot stretches her to the point of pain, and her moans turn into a feral scream, accompanied by her working herself on it. The movements are limited, tiny rolls of her hips as she milks the come from me. "Good girl, getting every last drop."

We stay like that for a while, my knot refusing to go down, but I make her come two more times by flexing my knot and pressing two fingers against her clit.

She cries for me. Begs me for more. And I reward her when a desperate little whine of my name slips past her kiss-swollen lips.

The sound undoes me. Taunts the wolf and pleases the man.

And I'll spend the rest of my life being worthy of my siren's kiss.

ALPHA KAI

EPILOGUE

You never forget the moment that changed your life.

The instant where everything you know loses meaning, because nothing matters more than her smile...her happiness. When a single color can anchor you—violet, the shade of her eyes, brighter than the stars.

Brighter than the gods themselves.

This is what I hold onto as another first rocks our world.

Her pain comes in waves, stealing her breath, and I wrap my arms around my mate, purring against her back to help ease the distress. She responds to the sound, the tightness easing just enough that she takes in another deep breath before another contraction grips her.

She stands at the shore, waves tumbling over themselves as they await their new heir. One foot on land, one in the water, and squatting while a special blanket blessed by Magda and Elara awaits the delivery. They'd placed it between her parted legs atop the sand, and the water has been respectful not to touch the blessed cloth. Water spreads around it, movements gentle, always easing back before contact can be made.

"Push, little treasure," I whisper, my lips against her damp hair, my thumb stroking across her swollen belly. "Push for me. I got you. Our pup is almost here."

Tears stream down her cheek, mixing with the cooling sea breeze. "I love you, my wolf."

"As I live and breathe for you." My voice cracks. Beneath my palm, my child shifts and moves, finding their way out. And beneath my flesh, my beast's purrs rise. His love letter. Happiness. Peace. Home. "By the goddess, I love you."

The next contraction hits as the last word slips past my lips, and my mate whimpers. The sound is full of pain, but there's pride in her emotions, too. I feel them through the bond. Excited to meet our little one and start this next chapter of our lives together.

She digs her nails into my arm, tearing the skin, and pushes.

My fate leans against me, not fighting against the pain but rather letting it flow. Welcomes it.

Her strength shows through each pant and tear—then, her expression changes. The wolf and I, we feel it too.

It's as if the world stops and the sea holds still.

"It's time," Nerissa gasps, half-sobbing, half-laughing as I leave one hand braced against her hip and drop to my haunches. With my other hand, I lift the blanket between Nerissa's legs and watch in awe as my baby is about to be born. "Welcome our baby, love. I can stand."

"I've got you both." Bracing my body close in case her legs weaken, I place the blanket over my hands and catch our beautiful, and slick, tiny bundle with little spots across her back in muted yellows and blues—her scales.

A little girl with hair black as night and a scrunched-up face slips from her mother's tired body and into my hands, changing my world once again.

Nerissa is exhausted as I place our daughter against her chest, but the smile that lights up her face is another one of those moments you never forget, no matter how many years pass. She takes in her face, counts each finger and toe, while I thank the gods for this gift.

My family. My pack.

Placing my most important treasures on a daybed near the sea, both for the mother's healing and baby's comfort, I send a mindlink to our family. *Little Miss and Mom are well. Going to call the midwife, and then I'll come to you.*

The announcement is met with a joyous chorus from our family back at the pack house. Howls and cries of joy, but I tune them out. Close the mindlink, and sit down next to my mate as a midwife comes to check my precious ones.

She's gone in thirty minutes, Nerissa's healing ability already repairing her body while my perfect pup passes every test. Won't deny I'm a proud papa either.

"What will we name her, Alpha? What does she look like to you?"

"She looks like a queen," I say, the perfect name already set in stone. "Attina Oceane Daire. Our little wolf of the sea."

"That's perfect." Nerissa's lips curve at that, tired but radiant. As if she understands, our daughter stops smacking her lips and looks up in my direction. Not quite a steady gaze, but there's recognition, and then toward her mom before blinking a few times. The haze in her eyes clears a little more with each movement, revealing violet eyes that flash gold for a brief second.

Wolf's fire flaring in her siren gaze...

"Did she just...did you see...?"

"I did." Chest puffing as the proud father I am, I bend and place a gentle kiss on Attina's head. "Love you and your mother, little one."

"And we love you, Alpha."

The gods may bend fate, but today they simply made room—for our blood, bond, and a daughter who will dominate both the land and sea as a siren and wolf.

. . .

The End...For *Now*.

**(Turn the page for some upcoming releases,
and news about this world!)**

MALETH...

If you haven't guessed it, Maleth is getting his own book in 2026! We will have vampires, explicit everything, and a sweet little beauty named *Crimson...*

More Info Coming Soon To My Newsletter!
Sign Up: https://www.elenamreyes.com/

Nothing tastes sweeter than crimson, poisonous and tempting. A sin you crave.

Elena M. Reyes is the epitome of a Floridian and if she could live in her beloved flip-flops, she would.

As a small child, she was always intrigued by all forms of art: whether it was dancing to island rhythms, or painting with any medium she could get her hands on. Her passion for reading over the years has amassed her with hours of pleasure, but it wasn't until she stumbled upon fanfiction that her thirst to write overtook her world.

She's a short and sassy Latina with an adorable pup, a kiddo that keeps her on her toes, and a husband who claims she'll cause him to go bald prematurely. Lol

Email: Reyes139ff@gmail.com

Newsletter Sign-Up:
https://www.elenamreyes.com/

Elena's Marked Girls.
Come join the naughty fun.
Link: https://www.facebook.com/groups/1710869452526025/

tiktok.com/@authorelenamreyes

facebook.com/AuthorElenaMReyes

instagram.com/authorelenamreyes

bookbub.com/profile/elena-m-reyes

pinterest.com/AuthorElenaMReyes

amazon.com/stores/Elena-M.-Reyes/author/B00E3E26X8

ALSO BY ELENA M. REYES

FATE'S BITE SERIES

LITTLE LIES

LITTLE MATE

HALF TRUTHS DUET

HALF TRUTHS: THEN

HALF TRUTHS: NOW

OMISSION:

PART 1

PART 2

COME TO ME (2026)

THE HUNT (2025)

TERO (TBD)

BEAUTIFUL SINNER SERIES

Each book is a standalone.

Now Live!

SIN (#1)

COVET (#2)

MINE (#3)

YOURS (#4)

RISQUE #5

OWN #6

Beautiful Sinner Spin-Off

CORRUPT

MY SINFUL VALENTINE

SAVAGE KISS

ONE RULE

(Marked Series)

Marking Her #1

Marking Him #2

Scars #2.5

Marked #3

(I Saw You)

I Saw You

I Love You #1.5

Teasing Hands Duet

Teasing Hands #1

Taunting Lips #2

SAFE ROMANCE:

Taste Of You

Doctor's Orders

Back To You

STANDALONES:

Craving Sugar

Stolen Kisses

MAKE YOU MINE